The Dorothy and Benno Stories

ALSO BY DAVID MILLER:

The Waters of Marah: Selected Prose 1973-1995. Exeter: Shearsman Books, 2005.

Spiritual Letters (I-II) and other writings. Hastings: Reality Street Editions, 2004.

Music while drowning: German Expressionist Poems, ed. with Stephen Watts. London: Tate Publishing, 2003.

Commentaries (II). Port Charlotte, Florida: Runaway Spoon Press, 2000.

Commentaries. Charleston, Illinois: Tel-let, 1999.

The ABCs of Robert Lax, ed. with Nicholas Zurbrugg. Exeter: Stride Publications, 1999.

Art and Disclosure: Seven Essays. Stride, 1998.

Appearance & Event. Providence: Paradigm Press, 1997.

Collected Poems. Salzburg: University of Salzburg Press, 1997.

A Curious Architecture: A Selection of Contemporary Prose Poems, ed. with Rupert Loydell. Stride, 1996.

Stromata. Providence: Burning Deck Press, 1995.

True Points. Peterborough: Spectacular Diseases Press, 1992.

Pictures of Mercy: Selected Poems, with artwork by Graham Gussin. Stride, 1991.

W. H. Hudson and the Elusive Paradise. London & NY: Macmillan & St. Martin's Press, 1990.

The Dorothy and Benno Stories

David Miller

With an Afterword by Anthony Rudolf

REALITY STREET
2005

Published by
Reality Street Editions
63 All Saints Street, Hastings, East Sussex TN34 3BN
www.realitystreet.co.uk

Copyright © David Miller, 2005
Typesetting and book design by Ken Edwards
Cover artwork by Ken White

Printed & bound in Great Britain by Antony Rowe Ltd

Reality Street Fiction Series No 3

A catalogue record for this book is available from the British
Library

ISBN: 1-874400-33-4

Acknowledgements:

The first two Dorothy and Benno stories appeared in *Darkness Enfolding* (Stride, Exeter, 1989), the remaining story in *Stride* magazine. "Blues for Pamela" was originally published in *Labrys* magazine.

"Darkness Enfolding" first appeared in the book of the same title (mentioned above), and in a revised form as *Darkness Enfolding: A Story* (tel-let, Charleston, Illinois, 1999). "Biography", "Round About Midnight", "Blues" and "The Serendipity Caper" were also included in *Darkness Enfolding*. "Voice and Name" was published in *Cards*, a collection of the poet John Levy's work and my own (Sow's Ear Press, Stafford, 1991), while "Dream Images of Life" appeared in *In the Midst* (Stingy Artist Press, Alverstoke, 1979). Earlier versions of "Round About Midnight", "Voice and Name" and "Blues" were also included in a booklet entitled *Out of this World* (Spectacular Diseases Press, Peterborough, 1984). (Some of these stories were first published in magazines, including *Plucked Chicken* and *Windows*. I apologise to any editors of magazines where other of these stories may have appeared, and which I've forgotten.)

All of the stories have been revised for this publication.

Acknowledgements are also due to Robert Hampson for his help with "Nightmare", and to the late Will Petersen for assistance with "Voice and Name".

Special thanks to Ken Edwards of Reality Street Editions for his encouragement and help in putting this book together, and for bringing it into print.

D. M.

Contents:

Clothed with a Cloud

1.

The discrete: contiguity re-forms the splintered elements, wind-ruffled water's surface, roads spreading out before us in autumnal colours. Something hovers unseen over us and tempts us to brooding presentiments.

•

Coming up the road from where she'd left her car, Dorothy was troubled – even before entering the old house.

A door, simply enough, opened upon a room with a corpse on the floor; as if she had already known it would be like this. She advanced into the room, and cried out to the figure she saw standing at the opposite end of the space. He vanished through another door, and try as hard as she did to find him, he would not materialise again.

And the face of the dead man. The long, heavy eyelids, and the start of a smile at the mouth. What would he have been able to tell her?

•

Before telephoning for the police, Dorothy had made a search of the house, constructing a map of its design with notations of any details that seemed at all significant in the light of what she'd already discovered. One thing that particularly impressed her was a copy of Frederick van der Meer's *Apocalypse*; it had been left open, and a shaky hand had underlined the following passage:

> Neither bleating nor complaint can be imagined with the Lamb, only silence. His counterfeit, the Beast, has ten horns stupidly distributed on its seven heads; it has no seven eyes, however, and sees but little.
> Roaring, flattering, insinuating, it works magic, hypnotises crowds and organises a diabolical cult.

She decided to remove the book to her car; then, having come back into the house, she phoned the local police station.

•

My worry, *my* puzzlement and horror, animated the space where the corpse lay. His lifelessness created a void at the heart of that space; and that void was the source of what I did and said and felt, to cover it over, and resolve the slackness of the ungainly slumped figure and the smile at the mouth which seemed to give a light to the heavy eyelids and the forehead. That stillness, that nothingness: I had to examine and examine again everything I could think of in connection with his death, in order to quell the silence which questioned and mocked without mercy my resources of ingenuity and reason.

Such were Dorothy's thoughts, as she mentally asked him again, What *would* you have been able to tell me? The mouth of the dead man hung open a little in that terrible smile, as if to whisper that death had closed its ability to attain speech. In Dorothy's mind she saw the flesh as a livid green – not of decay but rather of some unearthly dissonance, a discord heard in this world as an echo, much imperfect, of a blast of sound from some other space.

2.

Dorothy's trombone playing tended to remind me of Charles Majid Greenlee's: she had that same graceful authority and strength in timbre, phrasing and imagination. Strange that an Art History postgraduate from London University should also be such a good jazz trombonist. We first met in New York, when I was going around clubs and bars in a search for the whereabouts of the legendary vocalist Patty Waters. Dorothy was playing with a group in one of the clubs; and for a while we played together in a quintet, although my prowess as a clarinettist certainly doesn't equal her own abilities.

From where I sat in the kitchen, drinking coffee, I could hear her playing that Ellington classic, *Prelude to a Kiss*. Her playing – always reflective and strongly lyrical – today, unmistakably, had an inflection of melancholy, which I couldn't help connecting to her concern over the murder.

•

— Look at what I found in the house, she said, producing
the copy of *Apocalypse* and opening it at the underlined passage. She sat down opposite me and lit a cigarette. — You must
have thought this an important clue, I said. — Well, maybe, she
replied. — But, I persisted, you *did* think it important enough
to remove it from the house. — Yes, said Dorothy; you see,
Benno, I've always liked van der Meer's writings on Christian
art, and I don't have a copy of this book.

•

— What do the rooms afford us — ?
— As evidence?
— Trace; track....
— On which to home in.
— Yes, said Dorothy; on which to home in.
We were examining the diagram she'd made of the house,
and her notes regarding the various objects she'd found
there. I asked her why she'd concerned herself to such an
extent with what seemed to me the ordinary and even trivial
paraphernalia of the murdered man's existence.

— They tell us about the sort of world he lived in, Benno.
They're witnesses, and what they tell us may provide some
understanding of why this crime occurred.

She smiled at me then; and I was struck anew by her win-
ningly intelligent and kindly eyes, and her open, sensuous
smile. I'd always thought myself marvellously fortunate to
have known this woman, however much hurt my hopeless
love for her caused me.

My admiration precluded any attempt to dissuade her
from investigating the mystery. How useless it would have

been to say, This isn't your concern, Dorothy; let the police deal with it. For a start, I knew that the preliminary investigation hadn't left her feeling overly impressed by their abilities. But I said anyway: Is it so important for you to find out, Dorothy? You hardly knew him.

– I'd only met him once, it's true, she said. It was at Rose and Arturo's, about six months ago. He'd already given up painting by that time. Rose and Arturo were practically the only people he ever saw; he'd been an almost total recluse for years. Then he telephoned me from that absurd, decaying, ramshackle house of his and asked me to meet him there – when I knew damn well *no one* – not even Rose or Arturo – had been invited there in over a year. Don't you think that he knew something was going to happen? And that he wanted me to help him, or to share his terror, or at least to *know* about it?

– Rose and Arturo were away, she went on, and when he found he couldn't reach them, he must have remembered me and decided he'd have to take a chance on someone he barely knew at all. But he *did* take that chance – and I can't ignore that. By the way – I *do* think the van der Meer book may give us a clue of some sort.

I laughed. – Well, I said, I did *wonder* if you'd been kidding about taking it because you didn't already have a copy.

– And the objects, she said. You know, he was still arranging those bottles and vases and glass balls and things in the same way as when he used to paint them. But as far as anyone knows, he quit painting at least a year ago.

– Couldn't he just have left them like that from the last time he did paint them? I asked.

– I thought of that, she answered, but he wasn't the sort of person who simply left things around. He was too careful and tidy, however much he let that house of his fall to pieces around him without trying to fix it up at all.

– What connection do you make between the passage in the book, I asked, and the fact that he was still arranging those things as if he were going to paint them?

Dorothy stood up and shook back her blond hair from her eyes. – Let me think about it a little more, she said, and walked off into the next room. In a minute I heard her playing the first bars of Monk's *Round Midnight*. I put the kettle on to make another cup of coffee.

3.

It was only a couple of days later that Dorothy received a phone-call from her friend Rose, who had just come back from a holiday in France to the "news" that the painter Geoffrey Johnston had been murdered.

Dorothy briefly gave the details of what had happened: the phone-call she'd received from Geoffrey; her visit to the house and discovery of his corpse; and the shadowy figure she'd caught sight of in the room. She also told Rose the results of the preliminary police investigation, and mentioned her own tentative – and so far fruitless – attempts to find out why the painter had been killed.

– I'd like to come over some time soon and talk with you again about Geoffrey and his work, Dorothy said.

– I don't think anything I can say will be of any assistance in trying to discover a motive, Dorothy. Geoff had no enemies that I know of. He wasn't connected with any secret organisations – or if he was, it was a secret to me. And he wasn't wealthy.

– But of course, she continued, you know I'm always happy to see you, and I certainly don't mind telling you whatever I can. By the way, I have some journal-notes that Geoffrey left with me; he seemed to attach a certain importance to them – in as much as he asked me to keep them safe for him.

– Would it be all right for me to look at them? asked Dorothy.

– Yes, I'm sure it's all right. Poor Geoff, he was such a harmless soul. God knows why anyone would kill him. But I *don't* think I'll be of any help, Dorothy. And the notes he left with me are just some private musings.

– Well, I'd like to see them just the same. When could I come by? This afternoon?

– No, you'd better make it tomorrow. After three.

– Fine, said Dorothy. I'll see you tomorrow.

•

Dorothy's car was, as usual, being repaired; it was hardly ever available for use, but even when it was, it then often broke down while she was *en route*. So we waited, in a light rain, for a bus to take us to Rose and Arturo's. The bus stop was situated directly opposite a large public square, which featured a billboard-sized TV-screen and a nondescript abstract sculpture in yellow-painted metal. We were too far from the square to hear the TV clearly. The disjunctive appearance – the scale and the colour, in particular – of the televised images, in relation to the surrounding sights, gave a strangely dreamlike effect to the scene, an effect that was enhanced by the faint wash of sound.

The program being screened was from a children's educational series on modern artists; this particular episode was devoted to Marcel Duchamp. The format consisted of a number of cartoon sequences depicting various stages and aspects of Duchamp's career. Bemused and angry viewers were shown grouped around the *Nude Descending a Staircase No. 2* at the Armoury Show; after which we saw Duchamp selecting a bottle rack from a store, his act of will in choosing it being the medium of its insertion into an aesthetic context. Next, there was a sequence depicting the dust accumulating on the glass surface of *The Bride Stripped Bare by Her*

Bachelors, Even (the dust "breeding", in Duchamp's metaphor), as it lay on trestles in his studio, Duchamp later sticking down some of the dust as a form of colouring. The program also showed Duchamp painting the Chocolate Grinder detail of *The Bride*, the "chocolate" in question being sperm, as Dorothy explained to me. (– Messy, she commented as we discussed this last image.) Later sequences showed Duchamp playing chess, having supposedly abandoned art; helping to realise a gallery environment by hanging coal sacks from the ceiling and making huge cobwebs out of miles of string; and secretly working on his last *opus, Etant donnés*, gathering bits of décor from the countryside and from building-yards.

Dorothy wondered about certain images they hadn't included. She thought of Duchamp with his hair soaped into horns in a photograph for the cover of a gambling method, and Duchamp in drag, photographed for the label of a perfume bottle: the endless theatrical flair so characteristic of the man (his art being a form of visual and intellectual theatre). She also thought of the desiccated, cadaverous face of the elderly Duchamp. She thought of his statement, "We are always alone: everybody by himself, like in a shipwreck." And she thought of Joseph Cornell's dream of engaging his services in finding Delacroix's handkerchief.

But I thought of a trip I'd made to Singapore once with two friends, who insisted on treating the pitiful conditions of the poor as an exotic spectacle that existed for their benefit; and of my angry outburst when I couldn't stand their attitude – their detachment, lack of care – any longer.

.

Arturo, whom I'd not met before, was a small, burly man, stylishly and formally dressed, with the greying hair brushed back off the broad forehead of his pudgy face, and calm, serious eyes. He had been the first person to really appreciate Geoffrey Johnston's paintings, and had helped to arrange his first exhibition. Johnston was already middle-aged at that time, and even then he was reclusive and unworldly. Apparently his contact with the art world had been depressing to him and had contributed not a little to his eventual abandonment of painting.

Rose – a petite woman with curly brown hair, bright eyes and a ready smile – remembered one occasion in particular which had seriously upset and obsessed Johnston. He'd been invited to a party by a composer, a man who had been in Paris in the '20s and '30s and had known many of the European artists of that time. Geoffrey hadn't usually accepted invitations to parties, but this man had promised to show him his collection of artworks, including things by Gris and Arp, and the temptation had been too great. Besides, Geoffrey was, according to Rose, a somewhat naïve, unsuspecting person, and he'd failed to take the measure of this man. (– A snake, Arturo added about the composer; a vicious reptile.) What Geoffrey gradually discovered was that the composer had invited people who hated one another, so that he could sit back and enjoy the spectacle of a series of nasty scenes. But Geoffrey couldn't understand why *he'd* been invited, as he had no enemies that he knew of. Then he found out who his enemy was: the composer himself. This man abused him maliciously in front of a group of his young hangers-on, but as Geoffrey insisted (and this was what really troubled him), there was absolutely no reason at all for the man to hate him. The abuse was empty – based on no understanding of the nature of Geoffrey's work or what Geoffrey believed in. The emptiness of it was, for Geoffrey, the really sinister part.

I asked if there was any possibility of this man having hated Johnston enough to have been involved in his murder, but Dorothy remarked that there wasn't any chance of that, for the bare reason that the man had died more than two years ago.

– Besides, added Rose, I think he'd lost interest in Geoff soon after the party. Geoff didn't rise to the bait very well; however offended he was, however shocked, he was unfailingly polite and dignified, and that bastard was after a very different sort of reaction. And he had plenty of other victims; Geoffrey hadn't been especially important to him.

Arturo broke in to say that he didn't want us to get the impression that all of Johnston's contacts with other artists had been of this type; it was an extreme example of a particular kind of experience. Geoffrey did complain a good deal about the pettiness, egotism and competitiveness of other artists, as well as the bitchiness of some of them; but there were others he liked and respected and would never have said a bad word about.

– Of course, he added, he liked my Rose, didn't he? He smiled at Rose, who smiled back affectionately. – And he liked your work, too, Arturo went on. He always told me that you were the only video artist he really did like.

– Perhaps, said Rose. He told me he thought it would be a good thing if I went into doing video therapy with disturbed kiddies!

We all laughed at this, and it was obvious that Rose had not been offended by the painter's suggestion.

Dorothy and I were invited to stay on for dinner, and while Dorothy continued to talk with Arturo about the painter, I went out to the kitchen to help Rose with her preparations. Unfortunately, we discovered that a bottled vinaigrette had a suspiciously musty smell to it, after I had already poured it liberally over the salad. I went out to buy a new bottle of vinaigrette, and when I got back Rose was washing the salad and trying to wipe the dressing off with bits of toilet paper. (– It's all I could find, she said apologetically.)

Throughout dinner and afterwards, we continued to talk about Geoffrey Johnston. Rose and Arturo reminisced about him at length, and it was plain that however eccentric and reclusive an individual he had been, they'd both been genuinely fond of him. They also talked about his interest in Christian mystical writings and the probable relevance of this to his work. Two things emerged from this discussion: firstly, the idea of the physical world as a text which could be read symbolically or hieroglyphically, with a good deal of emphasis on Johnston's part on such aspects or capacities of common things as those of receiving, containing, providing, veiling, showing, enduring, and so forth; secondly, the idea of an interrelatedness of phenomena in terms of some sort of transcendent order or unity. Arturo pointed out that Johnston had felt that these ideas were in direct opposition to the dominant world-views that reduced phenomena to the level of sheer, valueless matter for the manipulation of the will. Geoffrey tended to see innumerable negative features of the modern period – the post-modern, too – in a metaphysical light; and he would occasionally disclose some very pessimistic expectations about the increasing, and deepening, negativity of the immediate future. His paintings had been an attempt at realising some disclosure of that transcendent unity he believed in, and as such constituted a counter-force to the world-views on which he blamed so much. But apparently, towards the end, his pessimism about prevailing ideological tendencies and the accelerating violence and cynicism of the present, together with his dissatisfaction with the art world, had paralysed him as an artist. This was, at least, the only way Rose and Arturo were able to interpret the inactivity at the end of Geoffrey's life.

Finally, Dorothy reminded Rose of the manuscript she'd promised to show her. It consisted of a nonsequential arrangement of notes, which Dorothy found to be very roughly expressed thoughts about various subjects, and certainly of no direct relevance to the painter's death.

I cut myself off from the others, & have stopped altogether now. I couldn't be *seen* to be opposed – I've been judged as the *same* as what I dislike so thoroughly & which I judge to be so wrong. Yet I have nothing else: I can *do* nothing else.

I've sought everywhere, going from the most esteemed works to others that are scorned or ignored – from Cézanne to Len Crawford, from Ghyka to Wroblewski with his *Art Alphabet*, from Goethe to Swedenborg & even Peter John Olivi. I've gone to *whatever* was useful in my search.

In the beauty of a person's being we recognise the adumbration of eternal life – the beauty that transcends death & decay.

Grace, to build. The city: unity of things, beyond totalization (rule of numbers, quantification, levelling of differences & individual values). Relation is *via* the Absolute (infinity / eternity).

Fate & character: the earthly nexus providing an opening for the action of supernatural grace; or in other instances, providing an opposed contrast against which the realm of grace shines in manifestation.

The senses: mediational & instrumental (rather than essential).

They open their mouths & breathe out ignorance & egotism onto their canvases.

Then I saw an angel standing in the sun, & he cried aloud to all the birds flying in mid-heaven: "Come & gather for God's great supper, to eat the flesh of kings & commoners & fighting men, the flesh of horses & their riders, the flesh of all men, slave & free, great & small!" How would the angel make itself manifest to us? I often think: through 'the smallest of us.' The humblest; the least expected.

4.

There was a golden tone to the light, which seemed to guide the predominantly middle-class, smart-set people in their summer clothing into orderly groupings amongst the trees, like an updated seventeenth-century dream of classicism. The unbroken white nudity of a small girl's body swept dancing into a space of more intense light, the blank, numb tonality so intrusive, disturbing, that she might as well been a glacier suddenly introduced into the scene. She joined a group of other children, dancing around the seated or standing adults sipping tea and eating cake.

I had gone to the park to attend an open-air concert in which Dorothy was a participant. While waiting for it to begin, I tried to make friends with a good-natured labrador, feeding it cake-crumbs. Its owner, looking across at the rather sloppily dressed, shaggy-haired, hunchbacked young man who had accosted the unsuspecting animal, called her dog abruptly away.

Gradually the musicians assembled for the concert: a fairly large group, with a female vocalist, saxophones doubling flute or clarinet, brass, electric piano, bass and drums. I was greatly surprised, when Dorothy appeared and came over to greet me; in as much as I discovered she was playing bass trumpet instead of trombone for this occasion.

The high-point of the concert – for me, at least – was during the rendition of *What Are You Doing the Rest of Your Life*. Dorothy stood up and performed a standout solo, every note possessing a beautiful and tender gravity, and firmly assured in its placing. At the end of the solo, where I anticipated the line to be resolved into a final tone or two, it unexpectedly continued in an upward-thrusting, sustained burst of notes. I thought of Coltrane's playing at the end of *Meditations*, but equally of Heinrich Schütz's wonderful cantata for tenor voice, *Eile, mich, Gott, zu erretten*.

And at the very end came another surprise, for the band played a fine, limpid arrangement of Erik Satie's *Gymnopédies No.1*, with its modest, graceful melody-line sung to the following words:

> The spinning shadows falling are like
> the threads of our life
> and they become the threads of our love
> (threads knotting our love).
> The circle's haze of movement is circles-
> within-circles when you have entered the Dance –
> when at the heart you have kissed the lips of
> the Queen of the Dance.

I remarked afterwards to Dorothy that if the *Gymnopédies* was obviously the work of a young man (Satie having been in his early twenties), those words were just as obviously the work of someone even more youthful. She smiled at me.

– You're right, Benno, she said; the young man who wrote them is, I believe, not more than eighteen.

5.

Dorothy was on her way back from the library, where she'd been trying to do some research for an article on Ruskin. Her nerves were strained by anxiety over her other research, into Geoffrey Johnston's death, and she had made little progress on the piece. She stopped off at a café for some chocolate-cake and coffee; but her attention was forcibly drawn to a conversation at the next table between a young man and woman, both of whom (it transpired) had just been released from a mental hospital. From discussing different possibilities of committing suicide, their conversation turned to the necessity, as the man saw it, of "eliminating" sectors of society for the good – if not of society as a whole – of people like himself, who had the correct ideas and the will to carry them out. He assured his companion that, although he hadn't started to "eliminate" people yet, he would begin by killing someone soon. – What sort of people would you get rid of? she asked. – Oh, he said, the inadequates; then the queers, and the Yids, and the niggers. At that point, Dorothy lost her temper. She got up suddenly and, turning to the pair, thrust the table into the man's abdomen, and then before he could recover she punched him several times in the face while his companion looked on in paralysed disbelief. Dorothy turned on her heel and walked out of the café; she was several yards up the road before remembering that she had neglected to pay her bill.

•

We met in the Tate and walked around the Turner galleries, Dorothy quoting for my benefit Ruskin's censured remark, that Turner "was sent as a prophet of God to reveal to men the mysteries of His universe, standing, like the great angel of the Apocalypse, clothed with a cloud...." Geoffrey Johnston's calm, lucid portrayals of mundane objects were a long way from Turner's visions of cataclysm and apocalyptic light; but the apocalyptic note in Johnston – his belief that the disclosure of spiritual vision or truth exerts a counterforce to the accelerating powers of subterfuge, deceit and violence – was indeed the light by which we now understood his project as a painter.

Adjourning to the coffee-bar (which Dorothy particularly liked for the chocolate-cake they served), we discussed the melancholy persistence which had, presumably, kept the painter's sight fixed on his collection of objects and their arrangement, even after he'd stopped painting them. So much had been concentrated upon them, as a sort of microcosm, with their symbolic properties and potentialities waiting to be explored, expressed. We both now spoke – I realised – with a note of affection for the painter; he'd come to haunt our thoughts and speech, enlivening them with his absence.

– Benno! said Dorothy; it's no use going on – I've failed. I've done nothing to solve the crime. I've failed him.

Tears began to run down her cheeks and the sides of her nose.

•

Sky's blood-flow.

Imagine an open hand raised with the palm outwards. And the other hand, slightly below it, clamped around the upper length of a sword-handle, the massive blade of the sword rising above the head with its strangely gentle, calm eyes.

Imagine, too, a voice....

•

Dorothy and I were in her flat, practising a two-part arrangement of Luis Bonfa's *Manha de Carnival*, when we were interrupted by the telephone.

It was Donald Wilson, an art-historian friend of Dorothy's. His voice was trembling and he had barely said hello when he blurted out: As one Christian to another, Dorothy, I had nothing to do with Pamela's disappearance – nothing!

Dorothy got him to calm down a little and tell her what had happened, and certain details began to emerge: he had been having an affair with a student of his, and after a vio-

lent quarrel she had disappeared, her room being vacant for
days now, the floor littered with bloody bandages. He had
looked everywhere for her, without finding any clue. Dorothy
suggested it was a case for the police; but Wilson flew into
such a panic at this that she knew she would have to go and
talk with him, at least.

Having promised to see him immediately, she replaced
the receiver. – Benno, how do you feel about our taking on
another case? she asked.

Blues for Pamela

Chapter One

1.

Dorothy and Benno were rehearsing in Dorothy's flat, working out a two-part arrangement of the Luiz Bonfa composition, *Manha de Carnival.* Dorothy played the melody on trombone, with Benno adding a clarinet obbligato, keeping to a conversational and almost hushed feeling – well suited to the tender character of the composition. The inspiration for the arrangement came partly from a Sandy Bull recording of the piece, and partly from Lee Konitz and Marshall Brown's unusually thoughtful rendition of *Strutting with Some Barbecue.* It was a perfect vehicle for Dorothy, with her reflective, "inward" way of playing.

They were interrupted by a telephone-call from Donald Wilson, an art-historian friend of Dorothy's. (He and Dorothy had pursued post-graduate studies at the Courtauld Institute at the same time.) He had barely said hello, before he blurted out: As one Christian to another, Dorothy, I swear I had nothing to do with Pamela's disappearance – nothing! Dorothy got him to calm down, and gradually it emerged from what he told her that he'd been having an affair with a student of his, and after a violent quarrel she had vanished, her room littered with bloody bandages. He had searched everywhere he could think of, without finding any clue to her whereabouts. When Dorothy suggested that it was a case for the police, Wilson flew into such a panic that she knew she would have to see him, at least. Having promised to make her way over to his place immediately, she replaced the receiver.

– Benno, she said, how do you feel about our taking on another case?

2.

Dorothy and Benno had only just concluded – or failed to conclude, depending on how you look at it – their first case. They had investigated the murder of an artist named Geoffrey Johnston; and if the discovery of either a motive or a murderer had failed to materialise, they had been successful in another investigation, which took over from their original quest. That is to say, they had found themselves deeply involved in an investigation of the creative and spiritual ideas that lay behind Geoffrey Johnston's work as a painter.

3.

Buridan's Ass:
They placed food and water at equal distances from the ass, and he died of hunger and thirst between them, unable to choose between eating or drinking first.

Dorothy handed the note to Benno, shaking back the blond hair from her eyes in a characteristic gesture. – It's in

Pamela Cotman's handwriting, she said; Donald found it on her desk after she disappeared.

Benno looked up from the note, into Dorothy's keenly intelligent and searching eyes. He felt helpless. – You think it means anything? he ventured at last.

– I think it's a parable about the advantages of making some kind of choice over failing to make a choice, said Dorothy. She lit a cigarette. – What do you think about that as an interpretation? she asked.

– Sure, said Benno. Sounds okay to me. But where does it lead us?

– I don't know yet, said Dorothy. Donald told me that Pamela had been upset or anxious about something, but he didn't have any idea what it was; he said their quarrel was probably not a significant factor in her disappearance. (She'd become very angry about the fact that he'd given her a low grade on one of her art history essays.) Nor did he know what the note referred to.

– So what's our next step? asked Benno.

– You'll have to let me think about it a little, she said, getting up from the table and walking into the next room. She began playing Billy Strayhorn's classic ballad, *Lush Life*. Benno put the kettle on to make himself some coffee.

4.

Benno took it upon himself to pay a call on Donald Wilson. It was not that he didn't trust Dorothy to find out the facts of the case for herself – if anything, Benno's admiration for Dorothy, springing from hopeless love, precluded even the slightest doubt regarding her capabilities. Rather, Benno felt left out of things, and wanted to be able to say he had done *something* towards solving the mystery of Pamela Cotman's disappearance; even if it was only to repeat what Dorothy had already done.

He had phoned Wilson to let him know he was coming by. As he walked from the station to Wilson's house, he hummed *Moon, Don't Come Up Tonight,* and then *Goodbye Pork Pie Hat.* Benno located the house, and rang Donald Wilson's doorbell. Presently a light came on in the hallway, and Benno saw a looming, shadowy figure through the glass, advancing to the door. He soon found himself looking at a tall, broad-shouldered man with a crisp black beard. Wilson had genial but sad eyes, and his mouth crinkled into a rather weary smile.

– Benno Lieberman, said Benno. – Ah, said Donald Wilson, I've been expecting you. Come in, Benny. – It's *Benno,* said Benno indignantly (he hated people getting his name wrong, as they often did). Wilson seemed not to have heard him; instead of answering, he silently led Benno up a flight of stairs and into his flat.

– Sit down, Benny, said Wilson. Would you like a drink of some sort?

– Vodka, if you have it, said Benno. And it's *Benno.*

While Donald Wilson was in the kitchen getting their drinks, Benno looked through Wilson's record collection: as sure an index to a person's character as Benno could conceive. Wilson's interests ranged from Mozart to Eartha Kitt; but Benno was disconcerted to find he had no Charlie Parker or John Coltrane, no Miles Davis or Don Cherry, no Sidney Bechet or Lee Konitz; in fact, no jazz at all. Benno could only think that Wilson kept the jazz records somewhere else in the flat.

When Wilson returned, Benno asked: What instrument do you play, Don?

– Actually, said Wilson, I don't, Benny.

– You don't play an instrument, huh, said Benno. Well, tell me, Don, where do you keep your jazz records?

– I'm afraid I don't have any. Oh, wait a minute: I *do* have a Herb Alpert record. Yes, that's right. I guess that's jazz of some sort, isn't it?

– No jazz records, huh, said Benno.

– Perhaps you'd like to hear some Herb Alpert while we talk, suggested Wilson.

– Thanks, Don, said Benno, but some other time. Let's get straight down to business. Have you thought of anything that might be of help since you spoke to Dorothy yesterday? Anything – however small it might be – that seemed unusual to you about your girlfriend's behaviour before her disappearance. Or anything else that she left in her flat that may help us.

– I take it you haven't made much of that note? asked Donald Wilson.

– We're working on it, Don, said Benno.

– Well, there is one thing. A short time – just a couple of weeks – before she disappeared, Pamela had spent a few days in Boulogne, visiting an elderly novelist named Georges Gorin. She'd been corresponding with him for a while, as an admirer of his writings, and Gorin had suggested that she pay him a visit at his home. After her return, Pamela seemed changed – she was withdrawn and troubled.

– This could be important, Don, said Benno. Did she say anything about what happened when she stayed with this guy?

– No, she didn't. I thought that was rather strange – don't you?

– Uh huh, said Benno. Could be something in this, Don. Do you happen to know this Gorin's address?

– I don't, Benny, but you could reach him through his publisher – I'll jot the address down for you.

– Fine, said Benno. This may be a good clue, Don.

Wilson presently handed him a slip of paper with the address, and Benno got up to leave. – If you think of anything else, give us a call, he said.

5.

Dorothy wrote a letter to Georges Gorin and sent it by way of his Paris publisher. A week later she received the following reply:

> Dear Dorothy Evans,
> Thank you kindly for your letter. I think we could better discuss things if you came here and stayed for a couple of days or so. You would be very welcome. Bring your friend along, if you like. I already have one house-guest at the moment – a young woman from Australia, who is engaged upon a PhD thesis on my writings – but there is plenty of room. I would suggest you come next Friday – there is a ferry in the early afternoon.
> Yours sincerely,
> Georges Gorin.

Dorothy couldn't make up her mind whether she should go or not. Why couldn't Gorin tell her in a letter whatever he knew that was relevant? Why did she and Benno have to go all the way to Boulogne to find out?

She decided to see her younger sister, Millie. Millie could always be counted on for sound advice. At this time in the evening, she'd usually be found in a certain gymnasium across the street from where she lived. (Millie had chosen her home because of its location near the gym.) Unlike Dorothy she had no practical interest in music, but instead had dedicated herself to bodybuilding. Millie had what someone once described as "not just muscle but 'muscle muscle'"; her physique had even been compared to that of the legendary Suzy Green.

Millie was performing French curls when Dorothy located her. Even though Dorothy secretly harboured a wish that her sister would give up pumping iron and learn the saxophone (or any other instrument, for that matter), she felt a sort of family pride in the determination and success with which Millie had pursued her interest in "physical culture".

With Dorothy's arrival, Millie quit her training for the evening and took Dorothy back to her flat for some coffee.

– I've started on a new case, said Dorothy.

– What, after the Geoff Johnston fiasco? said Millie.

– Forget about that, Millie.

– Beginner's bad luck, huh? said Millie.

– Listen, said Dorothy, lighting a cigarette; Benno and I –

– You're not *still* hanging out with that creep, are you? interrupted her sister.

– Just listen for a minute! Dorothy said.

– Look, honey – no need to fly off the handle. Hey, you're looking a bit peaked, kid. How long is it since you've taken a holiday?

– As it happens, answered Dorothy, I've just been invited to Boulogne. I was about to ask you what you thought about my going.

– Honey, I'm sure it's just what you need.

– Thanks, Millie, said Dorothy. I knew I could count on you for advice.

– Any time, honey. Any time.

Chapter Two

1.

After getting lost several times, they found George Gorin's house, in a small and pleasant street not far from the central part of the town. They rang the doorbell, and after a short time a small, grey-haired man with a florid face appeared. He opened his mouth and then closed it again, looking intently at his visitors and seemingly undecided whether to say anything to them. Dorothy and Benno stood waiting. He opened his mouth again, and this time he spoke the words: I take it you're Dorothy Evans. – Yes, said Dorothy, relieved at his having broken the silence; and this is my friend Benno Lieberman. Gorin adjusted his glasses, scrutinised Benno and Dorothy very intently again, and then turned and walked back inside. Benno shot Dorothy a troubled look. – I think he means for us to follow him, she whispered. – Well, he might *tell* us, Benno whispered back.

If he had proved distinctly taciturn to begin with, Gorin became flamboyantly expansive as time wore on. He led them into the dining room and offered them some anisette. – I'm absolutely addicted to it, he confessed to them, pouring himself a large drink of the liqueur. He also offered them bread and paté, explaining that they would have dinner later in the evening, when his other guest, Laura Jameson, returned from her sightseeing. – Charming girl, he said of Laura; I'm sure you'll both like her.

– Are you a musician? asked Gorin, commenting on Dorothy's instrument-case. Dorothy admitted to being a jazz trombonist, although, she said, she had never intended a career in music. In fact, it was through a peculiar set of circumstances that she began playing professionally. When she was at university, she organised a series of jazz concerts at her college. On one occ-asion she booked a band that disappeared a short while before the concert. Their manager telephoned her and asked if she could help him locate them, suggesting that they would probably be at one public bar or another that they tended to frequent – and he dictated a list of addresses to her. The members of the band, she explained, were notorious for hard drinking, and for not turning up to gigs unless they were (so to speak) chaperoned; they were, however, excellent musicians. She managed to find them, but they were without their trombonist, and had no idea of his whereabouts. Before she knew what was happening, Dorothy heard herself telling them that *she* played trombone. Although the band members were a little sceptical at first, when they actually heard her play (and she said that she trembled the whole time that she auditioned for them), they decided to let her "sub" for the missing trombonist. The concert was a success, and one of the musicians – a drummer named Bob Clark – told her that her playing reminded him of the great Charles Majid Greenlee. When it turned out that the missing trombonist had permanently disappeared (no one was ever sure what had happened to him), she was offered a place in the band, and even travelled to New York with the other musicians during the following summer vacation.

Gorin listened to this story with visible interest. – I suppose you like Charlie Parker's playing? he asked her. – Yes, very much, said Dorothy, while Benno nodded agreement. – *Poor* Charlie Parker, said Gorin. *Such* a sad life. *What?!* I knew him, in Paris, he continued, and sat back to see what effect this statement had on his guests. As they looked suitably awed (*Really?* said Benno), he launched into an anecdote about how one of his other friends, Jean-Paul Sartre, had wanted to meet Parker, so Gorin had brought them together. They'd met at a café in Montparnasse, and Gorin had said to Parker: Bird, I want you to meet Jean-Paul Sartre. – Pleased to meet you, man, said Parker; I've got all your records at home – I've admired your playing for years. – He thought, continued Gorin, that Sartre was *yet another* French jazz musician who wanted to meet him. *Poor* Jean-Paul Sartre. *What?!*

Georges Gorin, as it turned out, had known everybody, practically, who was famous in the arts. Dorothy and Benno were soon treated to anecdotes about WH Auden, James Joyce, Jean Arp, Yves Klein, Paul Eluard, Igor Stravinsky, and many others. It was a ceaseless flow of gossip, with at times a mischievous quality, punctuated by exclamations of *What?!* and accompanied by a good deal of drinking.

It was also punctuated by the arrival of Laura Jameson, a tiny, very slender woman in her early twenties, with a long, thin face, high cheekbones, an extremely large mouth, and long plaits; she spoke with a pronounced Australian accent;

and when asked if she played an instrument, she had to answer in the negative. But Gorin let nothing stop him for more than a brief pause. He prepared their dinner while shouting out anecdotes from the kitchen.

Coming back into the dining room to get another drink, Gorin began whistling what was recognisably a blues melody, rather rudimentary in character. – What's the tune, Georges? asked Benno. – That, replied Gorin, is the melody of the only blues written by Franz Kafka. *Poor* Kafka. I knew him in Berlin, in 1923; I was seventeen at the time. Of course, he died the following year.

– Kafka wrote a *blues*? said Dorothy, incredulously.

– Oh, Kafka loved blues, said Gorin. He had the best collection of blues records in Berlin.

– Isn't that impossible? said Dorothy.

Gorin looked puzzled. – Do you know of someone who had a *better* collection? he asked.

– No, said Dorothy, I meant I shouldn't have thought he could have had a blues collection at all.

Gorin looked shocked. – You think Franz Kafka was a *liar*? he asked.

Dorothy retreated into acquiescence. – No, Georges, she said; of course not. Would you tell us the words of his song?

– Better than that, he said, I'll sing them for you. *What?!* He cleared his throat, and began to sing. He had a thin, old man's voice, but he still managed to bring a considerable amount of gusto to his performance.

> You keep moving, but the Law'll be coming around,
> Keep moving, yes, that Law'll be coming around,
> You've done nothing, but the Law'll throw you down.

Dorothy quickly unpacked her trombone, and joined in.

> It's a dirty pity, and it's a crying shame,
> It's a dirty pity, low down crying shame,
> The way the Law will hold a man to blame.

Woke up one morning, with detectives standing by,
Woke up one morning, with detectives standing by,
I'll die an accused man, you know I wouldn't lie.

The meal that followed mainly consisted of fillet of sole
and salad. The fish reminded Benno of an odd and amusing
incident in his life which – not wishing to be left behind in
the telling of anecdotes – he decided to recount to the others. Sometime late in 1972, he had visited the elderly poet and
painter David Jones at a Catholic nursing home in Harrow.
They had spent several hours talking about a great variety of
subjects – Jones' art-school days, his admiration for Georges
Braque (which Benno shared), his relationship to Eric Gill,
and a host of other things. Before Benno had realised what
time it was, he found himself present at Jones' evening meal,
which was brought in by one of the nuns. The main course
was some kind of fish, which was obviously not to David
Jones' taste. He asked Benno to hand him a wastepaper bas-
ket; when Benno did so, he threw the fish into it. – Don't
want to hurt their feelings by leaving it on the plate, he said.

To Benno's relief, the story was a success with his host
and Laura (Dorothy had heard it before). Gorin expressed
surprise, however, that Benno had visited David Jones. (As
Benno had so far said very little – and nothing at all that did-
n't relate to jazz – Gorin wondered what his interest in David
Jones could have been. Perhaps Jones was a collector of Bix
Beiderbecke records; or had he played banjo in a band performing New Orleans jazz?) – Oh, said Benno airily, I'd
known various of his paintings since my early teens, and I
came across his collection of essays, *Epoch and Artist*, when I
was eighteen, and that interested me a great deal. A couple of
years later I started reading the poetry also. And then I
became friendly with a magazine editor who knew Jones, and
that prompted my decision to visit him.

– You hide your light under a bushel, Benno, said
Georges Gorin. *What?!*

Benno looked a little put out by this remark at first, but

when Dorothy gave in to the laughter she'd been attempting to suppress, he shrugged his shoulders and then smiled.

2.

– You kids get through a lot of drinking, said Georges Gorin, meaning *drink* (he eyed his depleted bottles of anisette and cognac).

Benno and Dorothy – thirty-two and thirty-five respectively, hence much older than the expression "kids" would generally convey – looked at each other sheepishly.

Perhaps with the idea of conserving his alcohol supply, Gorin took his three guests, late in the evening, to a café near the quay, packed out with night-owl teenagers, to chat and drink coffee. When Dorothy had gone to order more coffee and buy cigarettes, Gorin said to Benno, She's charming, isn't she?

Benno smiled in agreement; then he remembered something he'd been meaning to ask Gorin since their arrival.

– Georges, he said, what instrument do you play?

3.

Sometime shortly after getting to sleep, Benno woke up again and proceeded to cough violently; he continued in this way, with small respite, until morning.

When Dorothy came to say good morning, she found an exhausted and miserable Benno. Benno was used to the fact that he was vulnerable to sudden colds; as a result, he was annoyed, but not anxious, about being kept awake most of the night with a hacking cough – which fortunately had now become less constant.

Dorothy went downstairs and announced to Gorin and Laura, who were about to begin their breakfast, that her friend had taken ill. When she went back upstairs to see if she could do anything for Benno, Gorin turned to Laura and said: *Poor* Benno Lieberman. And *what* a pity he's a hunchback.

4.

When at midday Benno finally emerged from his room, after managing to sleep for a few hours, he was feeling rested and in much better spirits. Having missed breakfast, he looked forward to a good lunch.

The others were sitting in the dining room, smoking and drinking coffee. Georges Gorin was holding forth on Oriental religion and art, drawing on a trip he'd made to Japan for examples of what he felt to be the "minor" nature of Oriental art, and criticising those Westerners who attached themselves to Asiatic religions when, in his opinion, they'd be better off coming to terms with their own religious traditions. He stopped to acknowledge Benno's arrival (Dorothy and Laura both asking solicitously after Benno's health). The interruption enabled Dorothy to remark on Simone Weil's observation that Oriental and Occidental art can be shown to have many corresponding features – such as the use of void space in both Chinese painting (especially of the Song period) and in Giotto; and that parallels can also be traced between Daoist thought on the one hand and Greek and Christian thinking on the other.

– Ah, said Gorin; *poor* Simone Weil.

– You didn't happen to know her? asked Benno.

– We met briefly, he said, in Paris – sometime in 1938. Terribly neurotic, of course. I remember a friend of mine kissed her, in a playful spirit, and she burst out crying.

– Did you get a chance to talk with her? asked Dorothy.

– A little, he said. The poet Joë Bosquet put me in touch with Simone. He probably thought we'd have things in common because we were both Jewish. *What?*!

– Of course, continued Gorin, Simone was hostile to the Jewish tradition, to the extent of thinking that Christianity had more in common with Greek spirituality.

– You wouldn't have agreed about much, in that case? asked Dorothy, who had already become aware that Georges Gorin took his Jewishness very seriously.

– No, said Gorin, not much. In fact, he said after a pause, in which he helped himself to another of Dorothy's cigarettes, we didn't agree about anything.

While Gorin and Dorothy were conversing about Simone Weil, Benno had poured himself some coffee from a jug. He wondered at what time Gorin would serve lunch. As it turned out, however, his hopes were shattered when Gorin did announce lunch an hour later. Gorin simply told Benno he wasn't well enough to eat anything and that was that. Benno walked out of the room in disgust and went back upstairs.

5.

Laura and Dorothy went for a walk together while Georges Gorin worked on his new novel.

Dorothy talked about her experience of living briefly in New York, while playing with the band; she added that it had been in New York that she'd met Benno.

– I do like Benno, said Laura, but I suspect he's a woman-hater.

– Well, *I've* never thought he was a woman-hater, said Dorothy. What a strange thing to say.

– Most men are, you know, said Laura. They feel castrated by women. And besides, Benno is gay, isn't he?

– Actually, no, said Dorothy.

– Really? said Laura, looking thoughtful. I felt certain he would be. But please don't think that I don't like your friend, even if he *is* boring. Boring people, after all, are really interesting.

– No, she said, I'm sorry, Laura, but boring people are really boring and interesting people are really interesting. And *I* don't find Benno boring, not in the least!

– *Oh*, said Laura, showing alarm at Dorothy's obvious impatience with her, *you don't understand* –

– What's there to not understand? said Dorothy, losing her temper. You've talked a lot of nonsense and been insulting about my friend.

Laura looked completely flustered. – But I *do* like Benno, she said helplessly.

They walked on in silence for a while. Then Dorothy took pity on Laura, and asked her to talk about her thesis on Georges Gorin. The rest of the afternoon passed uneventfully, and they were making their way back to Gorin's when they encountered Benno in the street.

– I didn't expect to come across you, said Dorothy, laughing; I thought you'd be resting.

Benno gave her an angry look. – I want to talk with you, he said – alone, if you don't mind.

Laura excused herself and walked away, even more convinced, no doubt, that Benno was a woman-hating homosexual.

– What's wrong? asked Dorothy.

– You deserted me! said Benno. You never asked me if I wanted to come with you – you just took off and left me to it. And I've had nothing to eat all day – I'm *starving*. I came out to find a restaurant, but you know I don't speak any French, so what's the use of my going into one when I won't be able to order anything.

– Benno, you're being rather melodramatic, said Dorothy. I thought you were too ill to come for a walk. Georges didn't give you lunch for the same reason – though I admit I thought it unnecessary for him to do that.

When Benno didn't reply, she added: We could go to a restaurant now, if you like. My French is a little rusty, but I can get by with it.

Benno cheered up enormously at the prospect of a meal. However, they managed to lose their way in trying to find a suitable eating-place, and ended up on the outskirts of the town before they realised their mistake. Feeling tired, they stopped first at a small café for a coffee; soon afterwards, they found a restaurant to their liking, where they had a large and leisurely meal. Dorothy insisted on a course of oysters; she was especially fond of them, and had been attempting for years to get Benno (who had little interest in seafood) to try them; on this occasion he succumbed.

– Dorothy, said Benno, let's return to London as soon as we can. I've had enough of this place.

– You know, I think I have as well, she replied.

They arrived back at Gorin's shortly after Gorin and Laura had finished their evening meal. Dorothy apologised for their absence, saying that they'd gone for a walk and had lost their way. When Gorin suggested he reheat the remaining chicken casserole for them, they felt it impossible – from courtesy, and a desire to hide the fact that they'd already eaten – to refuse his kindness. He also insisted that they have bread and paté; and, as usual, there was plenty of coffee and alcohol. Sadly, it was an effort to hide the reluctance with which they partook of the meal.

Sometime during the repast, Dorothy announced their decision to leave on the early morning boat.

Now it was Gorin's turn to be melodramatic. – Benno will never get back alive, he said.

– Nevertheless, said Dorothy; we're going.

– Besides, added Gorin, if you expect me to come down to the quay to say goodbye at half-past one in the morning, you're expecting too much.

– We have to get back to London for a rehearsal, lied Benno.

– You're not well enough to travel, said Gorin, and then reiterated: You'll die on the boat.

Their determination won out over Gorin's insistence in

the end. The evening's conversation took on a tone of farewell. Laura exchanged addresses with Dorothy and Benno, promising to send them whatever details she could find of current jazz activities in Australia. Gorin launched expansively into a series of bizarre anecdotes about gay taxi-drivers in Tokyo. After a time Benno left the room (Dorothy presumed he had gone to have a rest). Laura decided to retire. – Take care, my dear, she said to Dorothy, kissing her on the cheek, and then went to look for Benno to say goodbye.

Gorin and Dorothy spent the next hour drinking cognac together and talking about such diverse matters as the effect of ageing on the sexual appetites (Gorin) and the early play- ing of Lee Konitz (Dorothy).

Suddenly, in the middle of describing Brice Marden's recent exhibition at the Whitechapel Gallery, Dorothy stopped speaking and reached into the pocket of her leather coat; she brought out the slip of paper on which Pamela Cotman had written her note about "Buridan's Ass" and handed it to Gorin. All the distractions – the endless conver- sations and the drinking – of the past day and a half blew away; this, after all, was what they had come here for.

– Does that mean anything to you, Georges? she said.

– John Buridan was a Scholastic philosopher, replied Gorin. The parable about the ass is always attributed to him, although in fact it doesn't appear in his surviving writings. *What?!*

– But what's the meaning of it? insisted Dorothy.

– It's to do with free will, he replied. The ass doesn't have the freedom to make a choice between the one equal need and the other. It's not a very realistic example, of course – *what?!* But a human being has the ability to choose – that's the upshot of the parable.

– That note is in Pamela's hand, said Dorothy.

– *Poor* Pamela Cotman, said Gorin. I don't doubt that it is. That parable sums up the poor girl's problem very well.

– What problem? asked Dorothy. What are you talking about?

– I'd been wondering when you were going to ask me about Pamela, said Georges Gorin. It's simple, really. She told me that she was in love with two men. She spoke of them both in a very idealised way. But she was caught between these two loves in such a way that she found it impossible to go on loving either of the men; because while loving one of them she also loved the other. Nor, even if it had been con- venient (and it wasn't), would she have been able to love them together, for she felt she must give all her love to one or the other; and she couldn't. So she loved both of them, and yet was unable to love either.

– One of them was your friend Wilson, he continued; I don't know who the other man was – she never mentioned his name.

– Donald said she appeared changed after her visit here, said Dorothy. What do you make of that?

– *Poor* Donald Wilson, said Gorin. Too insensitive to see that the girl was in trouble until the problem had come to a head. *What?!*

– So you're saying that Pamela saw herself as deprived of the ability to choose one man or the other? That her will was paralysed by the situation she found herself in?

– No, not quite. Human beings are capable of tragic choice, as well. If Pamela hasn't killed herself (and I'm afraid it's quite possible that she has), then I imagine she's living alone in some place where she won't easily be found. I'm speaking, of course, from the knowledge I gathered of her, and from my intuition.

– Well, Georges, said Dorothy, that's very sad; but you've been a great help. I'm going to find Benno, she continued, getting up and walking towards the door, and let him know what you've told me.

Climbing the stairs, she looked at her watch and discov- ered they only had a half-hour until the boat sailed; they would have to quickly pack their things and then leave the house without further delay.

Dorothy knocked on Benno's door. A groggy voice said, Mmn?

– It's me, said Dorothy.

– Oh, come in, he replied in the same thick, unsteady voice.

She found him lying in bed, his face colourless and covered in sweat.

– Benno! exclaimed Dorothy. Whatever's wrong with you?

– It was those bloody oysters, said Benno. I've been sick *so* many times – *and* I've had diarrhoea.

– Well, she said, it's plain enough that we won't be leaving tonight.

– No, said Benno; I'm afraid we won't.

– Never mind. Let's hope you're well enough to leave in the morning. Can I get you anything?

– A cup of tea would be nice, said Benno.

She went back to the dining room and explained the situation to their host, and without neglecting to mention her friend's request.

– It wouldn't be good for his stomach, said Gorin. Hot milk, *that's* what he needs.

So Benno was taken a cup of hot milk, which, as it happened, was something he absolutely detested.

That night Dorothy had a strange dream (which she was later able to relate to a memory of an old folk-ballad). She dreamt that she and Benno were medieval minstrels, who chanced upon the corpse of a drowned girl. They made a harp from her tresses and breastbone, and took the sad, grisly instrument with them when invited to play at her father's castle. When Dorothy set the harp on her knee, the strings began to sound by themselves; the ghostly tones were like a voice, a voice that distinctly shaped the words: My sister murdered me.

The latter part of the dream was not, Dorothy felt, in any way relevant; yet as a whole it seemed to her – however irrationally – a confirmation that Pamela was likely to be dead.

In the morning, when Dorothy looked in to see how he was, Benno told her about Laura's coming to see him the night before. He had just returned from the bathroom when she knocked on his door; he was pouring with sweat, and had forgotten to zip up his trousers. Laura was clearly embarrassed, and tried hard not to look in the direction of his fly. – It's been nice meeting you, Benno, she told him. – I'll write to you, he said.

Chapter Three

It was some five months after Dorothy and Benno's stay in Boulogne that Georges Gorin visited London. During this time, there had been no discoveries about Pamela's fate. Dorothy invited Gorin to her flat, to have dinner with her and Benno.

– I've written some music about Pamela Cotman, Dorothy told him. It's called *Blues for Pamela*. Shall I play it for you?

The piece was based on a contrast between slow, grave, quiet passages in the middle register descending into the lower register, and clusters of quavering arpeggios ending in falsetto-like tones, in some degree resembling bursts of passionate bird-song. Dorothy used this contrast both as a constructive device and as a dramatic effect – which she pursued sensitively and with ingenuity.

Her performance was applauded by Benno and Georges Gorin.

Benno asked Gorin, while they were having a pre-dinner drink, if Laura had been in touch recently.

– *Poor* Laura Jameson, said Gorin. Terrible case of arrested development. *What?!*

– Have you heard from her? asked Benno.

– Laura disappeared over two months ago, replied Georges Gorin.

Nightmare

1.

Millie lay still for a moment, listening to her own breathing, gradually becoming aware of the sounds beyond the door, and slowly coming back to where she was. She remembered yesterday's long freeway drive – the radio's music; the drumming of the tires on the sections; finally, the Santa Monica Turn-off and her first glimpse of the Pacific Ocean.

She eased out of bed and put on her dressing gown. She wandered through the apartment and helped herself to some juice from the icebox. There was no sign of Tom; he must have gone to work. She noticed a couple of photographs pinned to the noticeboard on the kitchen wall, amongst the newspaper cuttings and bills. In one, Tom – a large man in his mid-forties, with long hair and a straggly beard – had his arms around a young woman; she looked towards the camera, but her eyes seemed vacant, looking beyond the photographer into some unknown distance. The other was a slightly blurred likeness of a white-bearded, swarthy-skinned man wearing a turban. Smiling, he revealed teeth that looked badly in need of repair. Millie remembered that her sister had explicitly told her not to ask about a certain photograph Tom kept of an Asian man, under any circumstances at all. Millie was curious, but not curious enough to ignore Dorothy's advice.

She recalled having been woken early in the morning by what had sounded like a harmonium, but unless she'd actually dreamt the vaguely hymn-like music, she must have fallen asleep again after only a brief time, for her memory of it was slight and indistinct.

Given that Dorothy mainly had musicians for friends, Millie thought it likely Tom would turn out to be a musician of some sort. On the other hand, it seemed odd that a jazz trombonist like Dorothy would know someone who played hymns on a harmonium.

Millie went back to the bedroom and took a letter out of her case. The letter – which was from Dorothy – was creased with much handling, but she read it again. Dorothy's friend, Benno, had disappeared. He'd been working with her on a couple of investigations she'd taken on, in the role of amateur detective – the murder of the artist Geoffrey Johnston, and the disappearance of Pamela Cotman. The last time Dorothy had seen Benno, he'd seemed excited about something, but he hadn't wanted to talk about it. He'd bought a ticket for L.A. and had called in on the way to the airport to say goodbye. That had been months back, and Dorothy had heard nothing from him since. Millie was in the States for the bodybuilding finals in Las Vegas, and Dorothy had asked her to try to find out what had happened to him. Dorothy suggested that Millie look up her old friend Tom Jackson in Santa Monica, as Benno had mentioned something about going there. The result was that Millie had been invited to stay in Tom's apartment for as long as she wanted.

2.

Millie backed the car out of the drive and started down Ocean Avenue past the rundown motels, corner groceries and

cheap bars. She was suddenly struck by the difficulty of knowing even where to *start* to look for Benno. She pulled into the
parking lot at the foot of the pier. A steep stairway led from
the sand to the pier itself. She walked along the pier past the
arcades, the fish-restaurants, the bait-stores. There was nothing here to connect with what she knew of Benno. At the end
of the pier, there was a sign that pointed down a stairway to a
lower level restaurant. The sign read: THE BENNY GOOD-
MAN ROOMS. It was too much to expect anything from this,
but Millie decided to try it anyway. She went down the stairs
and slid onto a tall stool next to the counter.

– Hi, honey. What'll it be?

– Just black coffee and a couple of eggs, said Millie. The
woman turned and called out the order to a thin man who
stood at the grill a few feet behind her.

– Haven't seen you around here before, have I?

– No, I just arrived. I'm looking for this little guy I know,
a clarinet-player, with a hunchback.

– Hey, Bill! she shouted. Come on down here. This girl's
looking for Benno.

A man at the far end of the counter slowly turned and
got up from his stool, and came down the restaurant towards
her.

3.

Benno had been in the habit of lunching at The Benny
Goodman Rooms most days, having discovered the place shortly
after his arrival. But he'd stopped, more than two months ago,
and the staff and regulars had assumed he'd left town.

– You know, I thought it strange the little guy didn't say
goodbye, said Bill in a slow and thoughtful voice, leaning his
elbows on the counter. We'd gotten friendly, me and Benno
– sometimes, you know, we'd go back to my place and do a
bit of jamming together....

He suddenly produced a Polaroid from his shirt-pocket and handed it to Millie. It showed Bill – with a large grin on his face – seated at an upright piano.

– Yeah, we had some good times, Bill said. I sure hope you find Benno, sister; and let me buy you another coffee, 'cause of you being Benno's friend.

Millie was a little irritated at being taken for a friend of Benno's – she had never really liked him, and was only looking for the missing clarinettist as a favour to her sister; but she let it ride. She asked Bill if she could have a tomato juice instead.

Having explained that she wanted to think things over by herself, she took her drink to a corner-table, and sat back with her eyes closed, hoping that some new idea might occur to her. She sat there for fifteen minutes or so, and would have left the place except for something that suddenly penetrated her consciousness from the other end of the room.

– *What?!* – she heard; an explosive sound that, as she found when she opened her eyes and looked over in curios- ity, had apparently emanated from an elderly man with a bushy moustache, who seemed oddly familiar. Then she remembered the photograph Dorothy had brought back from Boulogne. It was supposed to have been a group pic- ture of Georges Gorin, Laura Jameson and Benno, sitting at a table together; but the image only showed Gorin at all clearly, with Benno's hand visible on one side and Laura's shoulder on the other.

Millie got to her feet and walked towards Gorin, who was talking with Bill. Gorin was saying:

– I suppose you like Bud Powell's playing, don't you? *Poor* Bud Powell. Terribly sad case, *what?!* I knew him, of course, in Paris –

– Aren't you Georges Gorin? said Millie, interrupting the legendary French novelist and raconteur. Gorin turned to face her, his mouth hanging open in surprise. He adjusted his glasses and gave her a long look, as if trying hard to place her.

– I'm Millie Evans – Dorothy's sister, she said, and Gorin's face broke into a smile. –Ah, he said, Dorothy Evans – *charming* girl. Shame about her friend Benno, though, isn't it? *Poor* Benno Lieberman – *such* a pity he's got himself lost. *What?!*

– I've been telling Mr. Gorin about old Benno having disappeared, explained Bill. Mr. Gorin being a friend of Benno's, you know.

– Did you see Benno while he was here in Los Angeles? Millie asked Georges Gorin.

– We met a couple of times in this very place, said Gorin. Of course, poor Benno was disappointed at having failed so dismally at trying to find Patty Waters. *What?!*

– But that was years ago, said Millie, who knew the story of Benno's attempts to locate the singer Patty Waters in New York.

– He tried again, though, said Gorin. But let's talk about Benno over dinner this evening – if you're free. I have to give an interview now – my new novel's just been published, *what?!*

Millie and Georges Gorin made an arrangement to meet later at a restaurant specified by Gorin, and the French writer left for his interview.

4.

Millie had spent the afternoon in looking around the city on foot. There'd been an unpleasant incident at one point: a man had suddenly stepped out in front of her as she was walking along; he was obviously intent on some sort of attack on her, and Millie had struck him across the throat with a karate-blow, sending him sprawling to the pavement. Not wishing to be detained, and possibly involved with the police, she'd hurried off before any onlookers had a chance to gather around.

Eventually, she discovered a gym that met with her approval, and occupied herself with a fairly thorough work-out. She'd intended walking to the restaurant, but she lost track of the time and had to take a cab to avoid being late.

Millie fell into a conversation with the driver about traffic jams in the city. – This morning, she told him, I was in my car, waiting for the traffic to move again, and I looked across to this other car and saw the driver shaving himself.

– Lady, said the taxi-driver, that ain't nothin': just yesterday, I saw this little hunchback guy, sittin' in his car – he was playin' this *clarinet*. Sounded just like Artie Shaw, that little guy did.

Millie had little doubt from what the cabby had said that Benno was still in Los Angeles. She questioned him further about the clarinettist's appearance, and everything he said fitted Benno. The puzzling thing was that he said Benno sounded like Artie Shaw. Benno's playing was more "contemporary" in approach; and the only Artie Shaw recordings he owned to liking wholeheartedly – she knew this from a talk she once had with him – were some of the Gramercy Five numbers from the early 1950s. She thought that perhaps for the cabby "Artie Shaw" was simply synonymous – in some vague way – with jazz clarinet playing. But when he said that Benno had been playing Shaw's Swing-period composition, *Nightmare*, her supposition was destroyed: the man did know his Artie Shaw; and just as obviously, Benno's musical concerns had mysteriously changed since he'd left London.

Millie thought of one last question. – Did he look as if he was happy? she asked.

– Lady, said the taxi-driver, that was somethin' you couldn't help but notice: that little guy had the saddest look on his kisser I've ever seen.

5.

If, on finding the restaurant, Millie was relieved to discover it to be an unpretentious place specialising in traditional Italian cooking, she was anything but pleased by her

first sight that evening of Georges Gorin, who was already
seated at a table towards the rear. He was wearing a white
shirt with a design of small yellow flowers on it, and when he
stood up to welcome her, she saw that he also had on bright
green trousers – the brightest green she'd ever looked upon.

Georges Gorin had recently been to see Syberberg's *Parsifal*
while he was in Paris, and he asked Millie if she'd had a chance
to see the film yet, adding that it was currently being shown in
Los Angeles. When Millie admitted that she only went to the
cinema to watch thrillers, Gorin's mouth dropped open in
amazement and, no doubt, disappointment.

– But it's a very erotic film, said Gorin. I feel sure you're
someone who's interested in beauty. Therefore, you must be
interested in eroticism. *What?!*

Millie put down her fork and spoon for emphasis, and
said: Georges, I can be interested in beauty, surely, without
there being anything erotic involved.

– I'd have to disagree, said Gorin.

– I can look at a flower and see that it's beautiful, said
Millie. Where does eroticism come in there?

– The flower can have erotic associations that are related
to its beauty, said Gorin.

– But when I see a flower, I don't *first* think of it as erotic,
said Millie. If I associated it with something erotic, that
would be secondary. What do you say?

– Granted, said Gorin.

– And there might only be this primary feeling for its
beauty, continued Millie. From admiring the beauty of the
flower, I don't have to go on to any erotic associations. Do
you agree?

– I was thinking more of human beauty, said Gorin.
When you admire a person's beauty, you also admire them
sexually.

– If I have a friend whose face I consider beautiful, said
Millie, or if I look at a very old person or a very young person and find them beautiful, there's again a primary feeling,

and in any of those cases it would be unusual to go on to secondary erotic associations. Isn't that so, Georges?

– I have to admit, said Gorin, you're rather convincing.

– And in fact, isn't there this same separation between a primary feeling for beauty and a secondary association of the erotic in *all* cases? Unless you first see a person in erotic terms – and then their beauty is a component of your sexual feeling for them.

– Millie, said Gorin, I suspect you're a Platonist. Your sister described you as a levelheaded, tough-talking body-builder with "muscle muscle" – *what?!* – but you're a philosopher in disguise.

– *Did* she? said Millie. By the way, she added, this spaghetti carbonara's very good. You obviously know your restaurants.

– Let me tell you a story, said Gorin. As you like thrillers, I'm sure you've heard of the novelist Cornell Woolrich.

Millie nodded.

– *Poor* Cornell Woolrich, said Gorin. *Such* a minor writer. Could never see why my friend Truffaut made such a fuss about him. I knew Woolrich, of course. When I was a very young man, living in New York. It would have been sometime in 1928 – someone introduced me to him at a party. Cornell talked about his *mother* all the time – he was quite a bore, really. One day I met my friend Hart Crane in a bar, and he told me about a sailor he'd picked up the night before, who also talked incessantly about *his* mother. When he described the sailor to me, I realised that it had been poor old Cornell Woolrich, dressed up as a sailor. *What?!*

– Are you trying to tell me Cornell Woolrich was a *pansy?* asked Millie, putting her fork and spoon down again. The man who wrote *Phantom Lady* and *Night Has a Thousand Eyes?*

Gorin's face turned a deeper red. It suddenly entered his mind that Millie Evans might turn out to be a "queer-basher". He looked at her biceps and panicked.

– Excuse me just a minute, he said, getting unsteadily to his feet with the idea of making a quick exit.

– Hold on, said Millie. Sit down again, Georges. You haven't answered my question. You're *not* saying Cornell Woolrich – the man who wrote classics like *The Bride Wore Black* and *Rear Window* – was actually a homosexual? Or are you?

Gorin should perhaps have realised that Millie was teasing him, but didn't. She'd been slightly annoyed by Gorin's condescension towards Woolrich as a writer, and – knowing about his own sexual inclinations – she decided to discomfit him. In point of fact, she had no bias against gays.

– Oh, Crane didn't say the sailor was a *homosexual*, said Gorin. Good heavens! They just talked – about the sailor's mother. And it probably wasn't Woolrich at all – just someone who looked like him. Or else old Woolrich liked dressing up as a sailor for a joke – *what?!* You can't call a man a homosexual because he goes out at night dressed as a sailor.

– Glad to hear you say it, said Millie. By the way – we were supposed to be talking about Benno. He'd completely slipped my mind until just this minute.

– Benno! said Gorin, obviously relieved at the prospect of a different topic of conversation. *Poor* Benno Lieberman. I wish I could help you to find him.

– You said something about Patty Waters when I saw you at The Benny Goodman Rooms. I know that Benno was trying to locate her when he lived in New York a few years ago – in fact that was how he met my sister....

– Ah, but he'd found out she was in Los Angeles! That's why he came here.

Millie pushed back a lock of her auburn hair from her forehead. She said: How did he find out she was in Los Angeles?

– I told him, of course, said Gorin. *What?!* During a visit a few months ago, I happened to hear her sing in a small club. She wasn't using her real name, but I knew who she was. So I wrote to Benno, telling him about it. She wasn't at the club any more when Benno got here – and I've no idea if he finally managed to find her or not before he disappeared. Though, he added, knowing poor Benno, I doubt that he did.

6.

Benno sat on the bed in his room and stared at the dirty, peeling wallpaper.

How many more times? he thought; but he knew he had to do it. He put the recording of *Carioca* on his battered-looking old record player again, and concentrated on the clarinet part. When the record was over, he shut the machine off and picked up his clarinet.

He found the final *glissando* difficult to reproduce – but then he'd always had trouble with *glissandi*. The rhythm was also uncongenial; Latin American rhythms were inextricably connected in his mind with Nestor Amaral and Xavier Cugat – despite the actual difference between confectionery of that sort and the vibrancy of Shaw's music.

Benno put down his clarinet. He had to admit he still hadn't got it right.

7.

When Millie returned from her dinner with Georges Gorin, she found Tom at supper, eating a plate of brown rice and vegetables, with boiled seaweed on the side. Tom explained that he'd arrived home late because of having to visit a friend in hospital. He'd heard from mutual acquaintances that the man had been attacked while out on a walk earlier in the day, and Tom went straight over to the hospital to see him after finishing work.

– Wow, he said (he always prefixed a statement that he considered revelatory with the word Wow), this friend of mine – Jim – was just walking along, you know, not doing anything wrong, because Jim's a good sort of cat, and this woman – who must have been some sort of *psychopath*, Millie – just up and chopped him across the throat, you know, with her hand – and poor old Jim goes smack down on the pavement and hits his head.... That woman must have been an *animal*, Millie; they shouldn't let creatures like that loose on the street.... You should watch out, Millie, there are a lot of cats in this town who don't have any higher awareness *at all* – they're mean, dangerous cats – like that psycho who attacked Jim today....

To change the subject, Millie asked him if he had any Artie Shaw records (she knew from Dorothy that Tom had a large collection of jazz recordings). Tom obligingly searched around, and came up with a handful of 78s, a 10-inch LP of the second Gramercy Five group and a 12-inch double LP of selected "hits". Tom went to his room to meditate, while Millie listened to the records. She was especially interested in the piece called *Nightmare* that the taxi-driver had mentioned to her. Millie found herself immediately fascinated, and at the same time a little repelled, by the slow, pounding rhythm, the brooding chant-like insistence of the reeds and – swirling over the reed section – the lone voice of Shaw's clarinet. The claustrophobic, at times almost hysterical, mood of the piece – if certainly appropriate to its title – struck her as odd, being out of keeping with what she thought of as the optimistic, buoyant nature of Swing.

Millie shut off the stereo and tried to think out how this music might relate to Benno. Even if she allowed that Benno's concern with a rather contemplative form of modern jazz might reflect Dorothy's approach more than his own, she still could not imagine him being interested in this sort of music. Whenever you got an idea of Benno's own inclinations, you saw that he was actually less conservative than Dorothy. He'd experimented with free jazz in the '60s, and you couldn't imagine Dorothy having done that. More recently, he'd taken to listening to the composer and singer Meredith Monk; he even bought himself a Meredith Monk T-shirt. (When Benno wore his T-shirt to a party at Dorothy's, Dorothy met him with the exclamation: God, Benno, she looks just like Laura Jameson!)

If the mood of *Nightmare* was to be taken as an indication of Benno's state of mind – and from what the cabby had said, this was entirely possible – then things had not gone well for Benno since he'd left London.

She thought about why she'd never liked Benno. She considered his clarinet playing to be lousy, although she knew this was scarcely a reason for disliking someone. Mostly, she decided, it was a matter of the way he was always hanging around her sister, as if he didn't have a home to go to.

Millie sighed. She was getting nowhere. She began to feel irritated at having to spend her time this way. Instead of searching for a missing clarinettist, she could have been lounging around Muscle Beach, displaying her muscle definition while getting a tan. But whatever she might think of Benno, he was her sister's friend, and if he was in trouble she felt she should help him if possible.

Millie sighed again. What would she do tomorrow? There were no leads to follow up – apart from trying to locate Patty Waters, in case Benno *had* been in touch with her, or checking if Benno was working with a band in any of the jazz clubs in town. Neither idea seemed very promising. Millie went to the kitchen to get herself a glass of milk, and then she went to bed.

8.

Millie had been woken in the night by a powerful beam of light flooding the room, accompanied by a loud whirring noise. The first thought that came to her was that she was about to be abducted by the inhabitants of a flying-saucer – but then she realised that it was the search-light from a police helicopter making a routine check, and felt annoyed with herself for jumping to such a fantastic conclusion.

After a leisurely breakfast, she went out for a morning run, hoping that the early exercise might prompt some thought of how to proceed with her investigation.

But the running didn't work as a stimulus. In fact after half an hour Millie decided to call it quits for the morning and go back to the apartment for a while. She stopped off for a coffee, and then took a short cut home – walking now, as somehow she'd lost the heart for running. At one point on the way back she passed a woman polishing her car; the woman called out to her, Hi, have a nice day. – You, too, honey, said Millie with a friendly wave, but the woman had already turned away. Shit, thought Millie; what *is* it with some people?

Back at Tom's, she read a David Goodis novel, *Down There*, which she'd picked up at a second-hand bookstall the day before. She knew the story-line of it from Truffaut's film, *Shoot the Pianist*.

Millie helped herself to some lunch, and then made coffee. She was wondering again what she should do next, when the telephone rang.

It was Georges Gorin, and he sounded excited.

– I know where *poor* Benno Lieberman is, Gorin announced. He's been put in jail. *What?!*

Gorin explained that he'd been watching TV late the previous night, and during a news broadcast he'd seen a brief clip of a familiar-looking hunchbacked man clutching a clarinet-case. Benno – for it was indeed he – had a manic expression on his face, and was being led away, in handcuffs, towards a police van. The news commentator briefly outlined the story: a brawl had broken out in a certain night-club when the clarinet-player in the house-band had run amok, trying to smash everything in sight and hurling chairs at anyone who attempted to stop him.

– I've been trying to phone you all morning, said Georges Gorin. I suppose I should have tried last night, but it was really very late, and I thought it could probably wait until morning. I'll meet you at the police station, if you like, and we can arrange bail together.

Millie immediately agreed to Gorin's suggestion. She had no idea of what sort of condition she'd find the unfortunate clarinettist in, nor was she sure how simple it would prove to bail him out. She was glad that she didn't have to face the situation alone.

9.

Held up by traffic, Millie arrived at the police station to find Gorin and a bemused-looking Benno waiting for her on the steps. Georges Gorin, with an efficiency that surprised Millie no less than his generosity, had already paid Benno's bail, and the clarinettist was now in his legal custody.

As they all drove back to Tom's apartment, Benno whispered to Georges Gorin, You told me we were "waiting for a friend" – you didn't tell me it was *Millie*. Benno had surmised a long time ago that Millie disapproved of him, and he found it hard to credit that such an unlikely pair as Gorin and Millie Evans had rescued him.

They arrived back at Tom's without any mishaps on the way. Millie made some coffee, and they sat together for several minutes in an uncomfortable silence. Benno held on to his clarinet-case with one hand, as if he were frightened it might be taken away from him.

Finally Gorin said: Benno, why did you try to wreck that night-club? You managed to do *quite* a bit of damage. *What?!*

Benno's face brightened instantly. – Wasn't it wonderful? he said, smiling with pride.

– But why did you do it, Benno? asked Millie. And where have you been all this time? What have you been doing? And *why* don't you put down that clarinet-case – we're not going to steal it from you.

The smile disappeared from Benno's face. He was being asked to talk about a terrible period of his life.

Millie tried to sound as gentle as possible. – We've all

been concerned about you, she said. Dorothy most of all –
she asked me to try to find you. She's really been very worried about you.

– Okay, said Benno. I guess I can tell you and Georges.
But could I have a drink first – some vodka, maybe?

Millie searched around in the kitchen and came up with
some vitamin-fortified wine, which Benno said would do. (Millie
abstained because of her training; Gorin because of the demands
of a refined – if occasionally eccentric – sensibility.)

Benno sat back in his chair, shut his eyes, and began to
tell his story.

10.

– I ended up playing with that crummy band because I
was hurt and confused, Benno said; I didn't know what to do
or where to go. Those guys helped me out; but they also used
me, and I'm angry about that.

Georges Gorin suggested that Benno tell his story from
the beginning, so that they would have a clear idea of how his
troubles had developed.

Benno accordingly began the telling again – slowly, and
with a certain difficulty. (Not only because of the nature of
the events he had to relate, but also because he was a reticent
person who was unused to speaking about himself.)

He'd come to Los Angeles to find Patty Waters, as they
already knew, and although he had eventually tracked down
the woman Gorin had told him about, she was not the legendary vocalist. (– Forgive me, Georges, he said, but I don't
think you could tell the difference between Patty Waters and
Muddy Waters.) Nor did he have any luck with subsequent
enquiries about the singer. This left him with the problem of
going back to London and admitting his failure to Dorothy.
So he kept putting off his return. But the more he lingered
in Los Angeles, wandering the streets aimlessly, practising his

clarinet in cheap hotel-rooms, and frequenting the Benny Goodman Rooms, the more he became convinced that he had failed in all the things he had set out to do in life. He had solved neither the mystery of Geoffrey Johnston's murder, nor that of Pamela Cotman's disappearance. As a musician, he knew that he was not in the first category of jazz players, unlike Dorothy. Finally, he had failed to win Dorothy's love. Even in choosing to remain with her as a friend, he was not sure he had done the right thing, for he felt that he could do nothing *for* Dorothy, in the sense of making himself needed.

Then one evening Benno returned to his hotel to find that his room had been broken into. Benno had brought few belongings to the States, and had acquired little since his arrival; but he did, of course, have his clarinet with him – and that, precisely, was what was missing. He had owned the instrument all the twenty years of his playing life – his father having bought it for him when Benno was thirteen. He was inconsolable.

He did, however, arrive at a plan for obtaining another clarinet. As he didn't have the money himself to buy one, he decided to ask for a loan from Suzanne Bishop, a woman he'd met at The Benny Goodman Rooms. She was a jazz enthusiast and an amateur pianist; she was also the owner of a small art gallery specialising in contemporary painting. Still in her early twenties, she was probably – Benno surmised – the youngest gallery-owner in Los Angeles. Benno took himself off to the Suzanne Bishop Gallery, where he found Suzanne engaged in a telephone conversation. He walked around the gallery, looking at the paintings while he waited. He stood in front of a painting with a monochrome background over which an evenly spaced row of vertical stripes of a similar hue had been painted, and over which, in turn, a succession of diagonal stripes in several different colours were arranged at varying intervals. Suzanne was saying over the phone, in her slightly haughty voice, *No*, I'm *sorry*, but I won't help you again, and that's final. Benno moved on to another painting

– a completely monochromatic work of a particular black which would presumably have been achieved through painting thinly on top of an underlayer of dark blue. It didn't impress Benno. Suzanne was saying, I've *told* you, it's your problem, and I won't help you this time. Benno walked over to a third painting. It consisted of a rectangular blue expanse surrounded by a thin grey border. He glanced at Suzanne. A tall, handsome-looking woman, she was wearing an elegant black dress, gold bracelets and high-heeled pink shoes. Her fox terrier, Leslie, was asleep near her feet. – Yes, I know you're in trouble, Suzanne was saying, but I simply won't do anything about it, and that's that; you'll just have to find someone else to help you. Benno left the gallery while she was still on the telephone.

There remained a certain fascination about Los Angeles for him. For instance, he was both amazed and delighted one day when he glimpsed one of his favourite actors, Robert De Niro, in a queue at a croissant shop. But small and superficial compensations such as this were scarcely enough to stem Benno's growing depression.

He began drinking heavily. This of course only complicated his mental condition; which was also made worse through an incident in the street one night. A man savagely kicked him in the leg for no discernible reason, shouting Freak! at him. After this, Benno's deformity worried him as it hadn't in years – he even showered in the dark to avoid catching sight of his body in the bathroom mirror.

From this point on, he began to develop what he later recognised as paranoid delusions.

These fastened upon the character of Dorothy, who had, after all, rejected his love; and also upon his failure to solve the mysteries that he and Dorothy had investigated together. Benno had always wondered about the trombonist who'd disappeared from the *Blue Cross* jazz group, enabling Dorothy to make her professional début as his substitute. He began to suspect foul play, with Dorothy as the culprit. Once his mind had taken this turn, it continued relentlessly along the same wretched path. Dorothy had discovered Geoffrey's corpse – or so she had said. Couldn't she have murdered Johnston herself and then claimed to have innocently come upon his body? The more he thought about this, the more plausible it seemed to him. Dorothy had pretended to be investigating the murder in order to cover up her guilty secret, and Benno had unwittingly made himself an accomplice in this deception. The reason for killing Geoffrey Johnston seemed clear enough. Rose and Arturo, he persuaded himself, had hired Dorothy to do it. They claimed to have been Johnston's closest friends – but Benno felt he could see through this hypocrisy. He reasoned that Arturo had become resentful and embittered that Johnston, whose work he had championed over the years, had withdrawn from exhibiting his paintings, and finally ceased even to paint. Arturo had been made to look foolish by Johnston's actions. Rose, for her part, had undoubtedly been smarting all those years over Johnston's dismissive comments on her career as a video-artist. It all fell into place. So did the details of the next case: Pamela Cotman's disappearance. Benno had never trusted Pamela's boyfriend, Donald Wilson. Just to examine his record collection was enough to recognise what sort of shabby individual he was. (Imagine owning three records by Herb Alpert – a fact that Wilson had tried to cover up by claiming to possess only a single Alpert album – and *nothing at all* by Lee Konitz or Charlie Parker or John Coltrane.) Benno saw it this way: Wilson, having found out about Pamela's other boyfriend, had paid Dorothy to kill Pamela and get rid of her body. Then he had arranged to phone Dorothy about Pamela's disappearance at a time when Benno would be at Dorothy's place, to add plausibility to the mock-investigation they devised as a cover-up. Again he had been used, used! Lastly, there had been Laura Jameson. Benno felt indirectly responsible for Laura's fate. He knew that Laura and Dorothy had argued, and that the argument had developed from some insulting remarks Laura had made about him. He would shake his head mournfully at the thought of this. There had been no need for Dorothy to have murdered Laura (for that was exactly what he assumed she had done) – and for his sake! He imagined that he would feel guilt for the rest of his days!

Such were the thoughts Benno had arrived at; and, he admitted, he was ashamed that he should ever have entertained ideas of this sort about Dorothy. Something of the desperate condition he had reached in time panicked him, and he sought help through a Church-funded counselling agency, where he had a number of sessions with a psychiatric social worker. One of the things this young woman did was to put Benno in touch with a bandleader of her acquaintance; Benno was offered a job in his band, with a new clarinet as the bait. Bait was, in fact, necessary, because of the nature of the band, which performed mechanically exact, note-for-note reproductions of old Artie Shaw performances, transcribed from records and tapes of radio broadcasts. As far as Benno was concerned, the result was totally without artistic credibility – Shaw's Swing performances were one thing, and Benno had an appreciation of their artistry, if not an actual liking for them, but lifeless replications of them forty years on were another matter. He took the job, just the same, as he wanted the clarinet; and he was also broke and unable to face looking for work himself. More than once the leader bawled him out for changing the notes in Shaw's solos. – From now on, the man had told him, I'm the only one who says what goes. The rest is just bullshit. You got that, Benno? Benno got it, but didn't like it. In the end he went berserk and attempted to smash up the night-club that had come to symbolise his creative frustrations. – The rest, he concluded, you already know.

After Benno had finished his story, Millie and Gorin looked at each other with relief, for it was obvious to them both that however shaky he might seem, he had substantially recovered from the wretched condition he'd just described to them.

Tom arrived home, and Millie introduced Gorin and Benno to him. Benno was pleased to find out that Tom played the harmonium; he suggested that they might do some practising together. Then Benno suddenly said: By the way, Tom, who's the guy in that photo in the kitchen? – Wow, said Tom, glad you asked that, Benno….

11.

After Tom had told Benno and the others about his guru, who was, Tom said, the One Living God, they all went out for a meal together to celebrate Benno's release. It was agreed that Benno would stay at Tom's place, at least until the time of his hearing.

A few days later, Benno was alone in the apartment, playing his clarinet, when he heard a knock on the door. When he opened the door, he found to his amazement that Dorothy was standing there; she had a travelling bag and her trombone-case with her. – Benno! she said, kissing him on the cheek. Benno found it hard to recover himself from the surprise of seeing her, but he managed to say, It's wonderful to see you, Dorothy, and helped her to bring in her things.

Benno was also surprised to see that Dorothy's blond hair had been cut quite short: formerly it had reached to her shoulders. (Occasionally she'd worn it in a ponytail.) But the change did nothing to detract from Dorothy's strikingly attractive face – with her fine-boned features and intelligent hazel eyes.

She had brought a present for Benno: an elaborately framed print of Turner's *Rocky Bay with Figures*. She was talking with him about it when Millie came in. After the sisters had greeted each other, Benno showed Millie the print.

– Nice frame, she said, but I've never liked Turner much. Too grandiose for me. John Constable's much more my sort of painter.

– Millie, said her sister, that's the trouble with you – you don't like Turner. If you could learn to appreciate Turner, you'd get a lot more out of life.

– Yeah, maybe so, kid, said Millie, reverting to the *film noir* idiom she used habitually – and inexplicably – with Dorothy.

That evening Benno, Millie, Dorothy and Tom invited Georges Gorin over for a meal. While Tom and Millie were busy in the kitchen, Benno and Dorothy treated Gorin to a new arrangement Dorothy had made of the haunting Gordon Jenkins ballad, *Goodbye*.

They took the piece at a slow tempo, and kept on the whole to a grave, formal elegance in their melodic interplay. Nevertheless, Dorothy had allowed both for the inherent beauty of Gordon Jenkins' melody, and for the opportunity of making short amelodic bursts of passionate lyrical playing on trombone at climactic points, over top of Benno's evenly placed clarinet notes.

Georges Gorin gave them an ovation, and Millie and Tom called out their appreciation from the kitchen.

For Guy Birchard and Anne Heeney
and to the memory of Pee Wee Russell

Darkness Enfolding

Chapter One

– No one even believes that we exist, Catherine said.

But Joseph knew that the statement was, strictly speaking, untrue.

He said: I've heard people mention your sect, just the same. And he asked: What are you, then?

– Blameless. Pure and undefiled.

•

Catherine was a library assistant at the university where Joseph studied.

Her face reminded him of a painting he'd seen in London's National Gallery, the *Portrait of a Girl* from Ghirlandaio's school, in which the beautiful modulations of line fulfilled an expression at once serious, yet tender and gentle. Her grey-green eyes held such quiet. It was this that gave her an aspect of sobriety. (As Joseph had cause to discover, concern would readily appear in these same eyes.) Shy, in some measure, she would initially lower her eyes when speaking to someone. If at times a spirit of ironic or sceptical humour revealed itself in her smile, there was evident warmth, too. Her small, slight figure; her fine-textured, chestnut-brown hair, which she wore in a ponytail; the grace of her slender neck – all these things Joseph found affecting. And her youth joined with them to quicken his affection.

Only her voice disappointed – to begin with, at least; for it was slightly high-pitched and thin.

Joseph had overheard her talking with a colleague, in a nearby café after work. – It must be your own unhappiness that draws you to unhappy people, her companion had said. If you were happy, you wouldn't want to see those people. She'd replied quietly yet distinctly: It's not like that. – What is it, then? he'd persisted. – It's because no one else seems to care, she said. But he still asked: Why should it matter to you? and amidst a sudden flurry of noise from a neighbouring table, Joseph caught only the word *bleeds* of her reply clearly.

•

– Have you been away? she asked him unexpectedly, when he brought his books to the counter. I haven't seen you for some time.

– I was in Dorset for three weeks, he said. My doctor's idea. I'm supposed to go away and rest every so often.

– Why? she asked. What's wrong?

– Arthritis, Joseph said; and he repeated: I just need to rest from time to time, that's all. He thought of some who'd assumed the term was for an illness that only afflicted the old, and had merely puzzled at it. But greater than the small worry this thought evoked, unease – submerged for some while – took hold of him, a combination of remembered pain and projected uncertainty. It showed itself in his face. Although she didn't reply, she continued to look at him; and from her gaze there was a flow of tender feeling, cancelling all distance.

The next time Joseph saw Catherine he asked her casually about herself: whether she liked the job at the library, and whether she thought she would stay in it for long. Then, having found his confidence, yet speaking too softly, he said: Would you like to have dinner with me sometime? She smiled, in her shy and appealing way, and said: Would I like to do what? – Would you like to have dinner with me?

And she said yes.

•

Joseph waved when he caught sight of her at the front entrance of the library. He walked up the steps, and stood facing her. It was a familiar situation: he had been thinking all week of what he would say, and now found himself without words.

She took the initiative by suggesting that they might go to a pizzeria she knew, and went on to explain that she was a vegetarian, which made choice of restaurants somewhat limited.

Flakes began to fall again, if barely (the ground was already covered in snow). But while they were still on their way to the pizzeria, the snow gained in density; they could only walk faster.

– Oh – *God*! said Catherine. The exclamation cut Joseph short, and he waited in silence for her to say something more. – I'm sorry, she said; but if you knew how I hate the snow!

– You *hate* it? he said. But why?

She appeared flustered – aware that her outburst had taken him aback.

– Well, she said, I suppose it makes me think of my childhood; I don't think I ever had winter clothing that was warm enough when I was a kid.... I can remember standing around in the snow, during recess, and shivering; and the misery I felt seemed to me symptomatic – though I wouldn't have expressed it like that then – of the unlovely and terrible world I was forced to inhabit. I know it sounds melodramatic, but when I see the snow I immediately think of how blood would look soaking into it....

He felt strangely upset, if for no other reason than his own delight in the snow – in laden boughs and, against a pale sky, stacks, mounds of white.

Like the rain it was a power, additive in process and effect; more so than the rain: for if the rain filled hollows it also flooded off roofs and every convex surface; snow settled and thus worked its change. Yes, he thought, it worked a transformation; like the crazy old woman he used to see in the street, writing Biblical proclamations in chalk on the trees – so that the entire trunk was eventually covered with white marks. Mornings when he parted the curtains to reveal a white and unfamiliar appearance where the familiar back garden should be, always drew a feeling of wonderment. At a distance the snow simplified everything, as in those black-and-white photographs totally devoid of grey tones; but from a closer position the forms of things were altered in various ways, the snow making level, uniform surfaces here, and achieving beads, nodules, excrescences there, while leaves were slurred together like a brief passage of notes played *legato*.

He glanced ahead: in the middle distance stood a small group of trees, isolated. The clusters of boughs seemed lines etched into glass.

•

Seeking out topics, he began with the college and those who figured in its life. – But there's only one teacher who stands out, he said, and went on to explain his admiration for Maeve Robertshaw.

– I didn't learn anything important at school, Catherine said, and I didn't find university any better. My parents didn't teach me anything, either. My one real teacher helped me to change utterly. I was with her for a year, before she moved away – she spent her life continually wandering from one place to another.

– And what exactly did she teach you?

– That we have to escape from all the things that keep us imprisoned: history, nature, the body.... She taught me to recognise in myself a contradiction of those things.

– I'm not sure I understand, Joseph said.

But Catherine asked him to tell her about his illness.

He had been anxious, in fact, that he might not have done the right thing in mentioning it to her. That she wanted to know, he took as a favorable sign, and held back nothing from the account he gave.

Joseph described his condition as it had been until a short time ago: his fingers were badly swollen, and one finger refused to straighten; knees, ankles and feet also suffered from swelling; arm- and shoulder-joints caused him a great deal of pain, as did the wrists – pain that would make him yell out; while all through his frame he endured aches hour to hour, day and night. The most simple everyday things – rising from bed, and dressing; getting to his feet from a sitting position; walking; taking stairs – all these were to be accomplished only with absurd difficulty. At the same time there was extreme debilitation (compounded by lack of sleep) to be reckoned with. Gradually, over long months, the symptoms dwindled in severity, and were no longer disabling. There remained some inflammation in the joints, and he was easily fatigued; there was also the possibility, as he knew, of a relapse. He also knew how dependent he was on daily medication: there were signs of deterioration whenever he neglected the routine of his treatment. But on the whole he no longer looked ill; and he was as glad to be rid of this mark that singled him out for curiosity as he was for the physical relief.

Catherine had listened to his account without interrupting him by question or comment; now she said: I'm sorry that you've had to suffer like that.

They sat in silence for a moment. Then Catherine said:

– You know, don't you? No good and loving God created this world. It couldn't have been God – it had to be some nefarious and terrible power that brought it about. Why

counter eternal good with evil, or everlasting joy with desola-
tion? But that's what happened.

– Can't you see that? she asked.

She was smiling, and he was thankful that she was. At the
same time he had no doubt that she was utterly serious. He
couldn't frame an answer; he couldn't even bring himself to
decide how much or how little he agreed with her.

•

Joseph walked with her to a small open park, a flat
expanse of snow with trees and bushes; she lived on the
other side of the park, she said, and there was no need for
him to put himself to bother coming all the way with her.

– Joseph, she said, I have to be getting home – but come
and see me at the library, and we can go somewhere for dinner again.

Catherine put her hands gently on his waist and kissed
him on the cheek.

He watched her as she walked across the park, her figure
becoming smaller, darker, more abstract; and harder to discern
as she moved further from the light projected by the street-
lamps that bounded its extent, towards the dark central area.

She turned around, waving her arms – no more in
appearance than a gesticulating stick figure now, pure sign.
– Damn, she called out; it *is* freezing!

In the distance, someone was practising melodic phrases
– simple, slow phrases – on a trumpet.

Chapter Two

He woke from a dream about Xenia.

She and her family had rented, through some error, the
same flat where Joseph and his parents were living; the two
families were forced to live as equitably together as possible,

until other arrangements could be made. Joseph was surprised to find that Xenia's family was distinctly rabble-like; their bad manners, noisiness and vulgarity contrasted with his parents' refined, genteel ways.

The waking reality was quite other than the dream: Xenia came from a polite middle-class background, whereas Joseph's family were self-educated working-class people – respectable, if unsophisticated.

She said: Don't pity yourself so much, Joseph.

He woke before he could answer her.

But he felt, and would have liked to have said to her, in the dream if not perhaps in any actual encounter, that it was despair that claimed him more times than self-pity: engulfing him, then letting him float adrift before overwhelming him again.

•

When someone permits their life to be a refuge for unhappiness, they invite rejection. Joseph knew this; yet he suffered when Xenia stopped seeing him. He had not concealed anything about himself from her eyes, anxious in their youthful uncertainty; and she'd accepted him, because she failed to understand what he told her. Xenia's generosity was shallow, though true – and soon eroded.

•

They'd met at a college party.

Joseph arrived alone. Maeve Robertshaw was already there, talking to a large-boned girl with jet-black hair cut very short, and a puzzled smile. Maeve said to the girl: Do you know the sort of thing academic philosophers churn out? You can't imagine how tiresome these people are. Nor how persistent! I'm in the position of having to keep up with at least some of their publications – and I can tell you, it's like wading through ordure. – Ordure, echoed the girl; isn't that rubbish? – No, replied Maeve, it's *shit*.

Maeve caught sight of Joseph and beckoned him over. – Joseph, she explained, I was just telling this young lady how *fascinating* academic philosophy is. Xenia, this is Joseph Dawe; he's one of my students, and *he* can tell you how wonderful it is to study philosophy while I go and locate some more wine.

There was, he noted, a nervous fluidity to Xenia's gaze; and in every aspect she seemed in fear of changing from a twenty-year-old, back into an awkward child. This quality, which might have irritated, immediately endeared her to Joseph.

He asked Xenia her subject area; and was bemused when she said it was animal bones.

– What are you studying? he asked. Veterinarian science?

– God no, she said, laughing. I'm an archaeologist.

Later, he was to see the basement room where she sorted through boxes of bones from excavations; while another student, working across from her, examined sheeps' skulls. There was a large pile of flints in one corner of the room.

And she once, when they were walking together, picked up a dead sparrow from the pavement, carefully wrapped it in a handkerchief, then slipped it into her handbag. – I'll boil it down to see what the bones are like, she said.

•

Holding his hand, laying her head in his lap, or taking his arm during a walk – the habitual small expressions of Xenia's affection were what Joseph remembered above all.

But he also remembered – for there was no way to forget – their "differences".

He was envious of the younger men she knew. In his own eyes, the sheer dragging of the years showed, too clearly, in his features – there was a weariness offset only by a combative look that appeared in the eyes and through the set of the mouth. He would also compare himself unfavorably with many of her friends, because of the way they commanded space with their physical presence; his own body was slight and narrow-shouldered, yet lacking in any compensatory grace.

He was self-conscious from the first about the gap – nearly fifteen years – between their ages. At times it was only background: other things worked more damage in their relations; yet these depended upon the years in his life constituting the rift.

Joseph's father had been forced as a young man to leave his hometown; its industry was centred upon mines that were almost exhausted, and prospects of work were too dismal for him to remain. Sometime during Joseph's childhood, floods had struck the town; and on a television-screen he saw the heavy rains and rising waters obscuring like time the few discernible, nondescript features of buildings. This was, for Joseph, the image of the past – and he felt powerless to prevent each new day becoming integrated into this image. Small wonder, then, that Xenia appeared within his dreams to accuse him of self-pity.

If she clearly thought (though never explicitly said) that he was self-pitying, he thought she was naïve. He'd once been talking about his youth, when he was drafted into the Armed Forces during the time of the Vietnam War. Xenia asked what it had been like. – I never went, he said; my conscience told me I objected to the war. – What a pity you didn't go, she said, I'm sure it would have been really interesting.

He had lost hold at the end of that war, when the optimism of his generation dissipated itself. When he and his friends had been jailed, or attacked in the streets during demonstrations, they took it for granted that they knew and upheld some form of moral clarity. (He still believed such clarity was possible; but he could find no firm location for it in any exterior faction, nor within the details of his own living.) He left the country of his birth. He decided to become a writer; and found he had too little talent. For a time, he drank heavily – but that didn't last, either.

•

Joseph and Xenia sat on the station platform, Joseph wearing both his own scarf and Xenia's, shivering with cold that he alone felt. When they reached his flat, he collapsed into bed, feverish; and upon waking the next day he was shocked to find how weak he was, and how painful it was to move his limbs. Over the next few months these attacks occurred at frequent intervals. When they ceased, the exhaustion continued, and so did the stiffness and pain.

He had fallen into a long illness. By the time that this became evident, Xenia had already left him.

Chapter Three

– Joe, you always do that, Catherine said; you look at the sky (she meant the ceiling) or you look at your feet.

Then she said: I'd already invented your history for you. Of course, it wasn't *exactly* what you've told me....

She'd spoken of herself, too – telling him of the evening of her confirmation. The ceremony was held in a white-painted room, where she afterwards met, once every month, with others of her faith. She had sworn compassion for every being caught up in suffering. She had, at the same time, foresworn sexual relations. (And this – curiously, perhaps – didn't surprise or shock; Joseph only wondered achingly at how he could order his feelings to allow for its integration.

(A friend had once written to him, "Armstrong, 1929 and 'Some of those Days'. What was the tone they read in the blues? Of the loneliness which never knew words? Of the peculiar joy one senses in that loneliness (not happiness but the love which surpasses such – for only the lonely know what love is, that love cannot be found in the sweat glands, pores and hair)." Those words represented a particular horizon of feeling, the integrity of which he never doubted from the very first reading – however obscure the feeling appeared to him. In a similar way, he was drawn toward some process of integration; to simply reject his friend's words would have been inadmissible. Yet he couldn't decide whether this was because they called forth – awakened – something in himself, so strong it could not be refused; or because he wanted to disallow any intervention of distance between himself and his friend.)

He would have found it unbearable to doubt Catherine's sincerity, or her right to that sincerity.

•

While withholding his accord at certain points of belief, he felt sympathy for Catherine in all she said. It was as if a spirit of negation (to her eyes) preceded and informed existence. This demanded a further negation in response. He could admit the force in Catherine's belief that the human spirit only suffers in the body. That nothing spiritual shows itself in nature, was more difficult to accept. But Joseph admitted to himself that there were days when even a profusion of flowers appeared monstrous, a diseased condition. And it was true: harmony and splendour were mocked by disorder, suffering and horror. What surprised – impressed him, too – was that her convictions didn't bring her to despair.

•

Joseph's thoughts sometimes returned to what he had overheard of Catherine's conversation with the college librarian; and he wanted to ask, What about your friends?

But he never asked, and she didn't (for whatever reason) mention any friends.

In the same way, he didn't ask about her fellow believers, nor did she make more than the occasional passing reference to any of them.

She gave the impression of someone solitary.

•

Apart from the librarian at the college, Joseph had only once glimpsed a friend of hers, and that was by accident. He and Catherine were at dinner, in a Chinese restaurant close to her flat. A small group – Joseph recognised some as students from his college – occupied two tables at the back of the restaurant. They were playing charades, and Joseph called Catherine's attention to one young man – with handsome, intelligent features, and a flamboyant air – who was miming some unrecognisable action. – Oh, I know him! Catherine said, and went over to speak with him.

– That was Mickey, she said on her return. He was supposed to have been a keeper in a safari park; he was feeding a giraffe, while shouting to visitors through a megaphone, to keep them away.

– Where do you know him from? Joseph asked.

But she merely said: Oh, he's just someone at the university, Joseph; and he was not mentioned again.

•

She seemed oddly drawn towards the 1930s and '40s. The only time they went to the movies together, she'd insisted upon their seeing *Bringing Up Baby* – because, she said, she liked the idea of a comedy with Cary Grant, Katherine Hepburn and a leopard in the starring roles. She also admitted a fondness for *noir* films of the forties; and she had an *avid weakness* (as she put it herself) for their fictional counterparts: novels by writers as diverse as Chandler, Woolrich and Graham Greene.

Her small flat held few possessions. There was, however, a stereo; and she had a collection of jazz recordings that centred upon those same decades.

•

It was her Billie Holiday records that, more than anything else, they liked to listen to together.

Scarcely anyone believes the sentiments of the songs Billie Holiday sang – they're thought to be mere gilding for a more realistic love. Her singing (Joseph felt) was informed by the quality of her belief. The unhappiness of unrequited love absorbed into the greater pleasure of love itself, equally, the beloved's faults redeemed by the sheer fact of their being loved – this quixotic devotion to an ideal, so often involving a descent into degradation and unqualified hurt, can be an extremely moving quality in a person, perhaps especially when it's confused with warmth of feeling and sensuality.

•

Catherine asked Joseph if he knew an old ballad, called "These Hours without You". – Yes, of course, he said, it's a favourite of mine; and he sang it for her softly:

> Can it be true that I wake
> To these hours without you?
> I sleep and dream a dream to share.
>
> All the lonely day I don't dare
> To even speak your name. For I love you:
> I'd forsake the world for your sake.

•

They were listening to Billie Holiday singing "Don't Explain", and suddenly, echoing the words that had just been sung:

– You're my joy, Catherine said.

– And pain? he said, completing the line.

– No, she said; no. She kissed his hand.

Held by her gaze, he was willing to believe that some unknown grace resided in him, obedient to her eyes.

The instinct of love for her leapt up; but where could it lead?

He thought of the room with the white walls, as she had described it for him: bare of all but a table draped with white linen, lit candles, and a bowl of water in which the faithful ritually washed their hands. To deny passion its indulgences, while cultivating compassion.... He could not imagine Catherine ever lacking in compassion. It suffused her glances; and it flecked her voice with warmth, making it seem more resonant than he had at first thought. But to bring forth compassion.... Was it because the needs of others, specific individuals with particular needs, provoked some invisible fructification? Her joy.... *You're my joy*. The phrase transfixed him.

•

He'd stayed, talking, until late; and it was raining: so that Catherine suggested he sleep at her place and return home the next morning.

Joseph washed in the bathroom while Catherine improvised his bed from cushions and blankets. The thought touched him that she might, after all, desire intimacy; his better judgement dismissed the notion almost as soon as it had appeared. He knocked on the bedroom door and she called out for him to come in. The room was in darkness, but he saw in the light from the hallway, as he stood at the threshold, that she was in bed, and that his makeshift bed had been arranged at a short distance parallel to her own. He closed the door and traversed the remembered space; pulled off trousers, socks and shirt; and slid under the blankets. He lay beneath the sloping skylight, closed off by a blind; the rain beat against the glass with a sound like the crepitation of burning wood.

The obscurity was instinct with Catherine's presence, because she had entered into it. His eyes sought and missed her lineaments the darkness absorbed. So that the dark was claimed as a second face: it was Catherine's face, yet it resisted perception. And it flashed into his mind that this face was surmounted by a crown of splendour, which was also part of the dark.

•

Maeve Robertshaw had said to Joseph: the divine was revealed through the human face. Catherine would probably have asked, sceptically, if a face could be perfect and wounded. For Catherine, the divine might have been symbolised by the upmost flames that dissociate themselves from the body of a fire, suspending themselves in air briefly before disappearing. Or a bird flying upwards, redeemed from the earth; perfect and whole.

Maeve had asked – or said – in one of her lectures: What is it in the human face that claims a further space – a space that is always beyond our wish and ability to comprehend it? How to say, as Levinas says, that this space is the ethical?

But Catherine told Joseph, You need to close your eyes when you stand before another person, if you really want to enter into their presence. Joseph repeated this to Maeve; she crinkled her nose in irritation, and lifted her elegant hands as if to wave the unwanted notion away. – Oh how *boring*! she said.

With his eyes open, yet in darkness, Joseph discovered what Catherine had meant.

Chapter Four

He was standing in the college bar, when someone slapped him on the shoulder. He turned his head and saw that it was Catherine's friend, the young man who had been playing charades in the restaurant.

– Do you remember me? Mickey said. I'm sorry I didn't

come over and introduce myself that evening – but I always suspect Catherine wants to protect other people from me.

– Yes, I remember you, said Joseph – but what do you mean? Are you serious?

– Well, half-serious, let's say. I'm sure that I'm decadent in her eyes!

Joseph wondered if he was supposed to feel embarrassed. He said: I'll buy you a drink, if you'll explain what you mean by saying that.

– God, said Mickey. Only *one* drink? But let's go somewhere else. I know a much better place than this....

•

Although Joseph had never been inside a gay bar before, it wasn't at all difficult for him to recognise, not merely a number of those very flamboyant gay men, with their obvious affectations of speech and gesture, but also several male prostitutes.

– Anywhere else in Europe, Mickey said, I could have taken you to a place where there'd be back rooms for doing all manner of things.

– What in particular? Joseph asked.

– Oh, *Joseph*, use your imagination!

Joseph thought it significant that Mickey chose to be apologetic: the bar indeed seemed an anticlimax. Catherine's regard for "blamelessness" (as she called it) was far removed from anything priggish. As if in reply to Joseph's thoughts, Mickey said:

– I don't want you to misunderstand; Catherine's always stopped short of any *open* disapproval of the way I live – and as you can see, I'm not *afraid* of anyone disapproving. It's those beliefs of hers that I mean! I was so shocked when she first told me about them, I kicked a couple of phone-boxes on the way home, to let off some emotion.

– You think she's intolerant? Joseph asked.

– Well, she doesn't act as if she were; and God knows, she's as kind as anyone I've ever met. It's her ideas – they're so strict and severe and bleak. And for heaven's sake, the girl doesn't believe in sex!

A tall woman with peroxide-blonde hair and heavy black mascara came over to their table to ask for a light. Joseph had noticed her when he first came into the bar – for she was the only woman there. She rejoined her companion, a pudgy man in a business suit. Joseph heard him say to her: We can go anywhere you like, I'll take you to the best restaurant in town. – She's a prostitute, isn't she? Joseph said to Mickey; not because he was uncertain of it, or because he felt Mickey needed to be told, but as an idle comment to fill a gap in the conversation. Mickey looked at him incredulously. – *He*, Joseph, not *she*; and he giggled at Joseph's naivety.

– I'll tell you about an incident I once witnessed, Mickey said; it might give you a different insight into our friend Catherine. He raised a hand. – Oh, it's nothing that reflects badly on her; don't worry, it's not *that* sort of story!

He told Joseph that he and Catherine had dined together one evening; after their meal, Catherine suggested a walk. They were walking with no particular destination in mind, and eventually found themselves lost, wandering streets of which they lacked comprehension. But neither of them felt this a cause for concern. They sat down on a public bench, and she suggested they tried talking to passers-by and see what happened. It was beginning to get dark. As a man walked past, Catherine shyly smiled and said hello; the man either didn't hear or chose to ignore her. – Your turn, she said. This time a dog came by, and Mickey called to it. The dog came up to him, all curiosity and friendliness. – That's not exactly fair, she said; I meant *humans*.

– So much, said Mickey, for what I'll call the prelude to this story.

– We set off again, he continued; in time we found ourselves at a pub, and Catherine agreed to go in with me. I went to order at the bar, and who should I see? A really obnoxious guy from the college, named Johnny. Do you know the guy I mean? No? Well, you wouldn't want to. He once pointed out a girl that he had the hots for, and said: Wouldn't it be *really* exciting to cut her breasts off? I could see that he meant it, as well.

– He didn't spot me at the bar, and I returned to Catherine as quickly as possible. We talked for a while, and then I went to take a leak. When I got back, I saw that Johnny had seated himself at our table; he was holding forth to Catherine in a drunken, nasty fashion. He didn't even bother to acknowledge me, the creep, but just carried on as if I wasn't there. I felt like pissing in his lap – it made me regret I'd just been.
– The more arbitrary your desires, he was saying, the better. I want to crap on conventions –

– That's not the point, said Catherine.

– What? he snapped at her.

– Conventions, she said. They're not the real issue –

– I can do anything, he broke in, that I wish to – rape, steal, murder, if I choose – and do you know why? Because there's nothing more sovereign than my will. Asserting my will to the utmost, I become God – the only God there is.

– Catherine turned to me, Mickey continued; she said, I thought you meant *humans*. Of course, I knew exactly what she was referring to, and I started giggling.

– What's funny? Johnny said. Are you going to let me in on the joke?

– You said you were God, Catherine said, but you're not even God's snot; that's the joke.

– So help me, Mickey said to Joseph. Well, I was in stitches; he was *so* angry. But I confess it surprised me, at the same time, to hear Catherine come out with such a thing. Johnny went off cursing us both, *rather* loudly; and Catherine touched my arm, and said:

– Nothing impure is worthy of the name of God.

– You were surprised, Joseph said, because she's always so gentle?

– Mmn, said Mickey. That's it.

– Later, he continued, we talked a little about Johnny, and I mentioned his comment about the girl's breasts. Of course, she was disgusted. But then she told me about Saint Agatha...

– She refused to sacrifice her virginity to a lecherous and powerful lord, said Joseph; he had her breasts cut off.

– Yes. And I began to say, Well, if you believed in what Catholicism taught – and that was as much as I managed to get out. – But the Church! Catherine said. I can tell you the story of a girl who refused to lose her virginity to a cleric – this happened in the twelfth century – and she was burned at the stake as a heretic.

•

– A small and unsteady light, Joseph said, wrested from utter abandonment.

He and Mickey watched as a Down's syndrome girl – with joy in her eyes – ran down a passage of the underground, her companion calling after her in vain.

– Eurydice would run like that, Joseph said, past the multitudes that could be barely sensed along the dark corridors of the Underworld.

•

– What else have you got to drink? asked Mickey. Joseph had invited him back "for a nightcap" – and Mickey had quickly worked his way through whatever remained of bottles of whisky, gin and vodka.

– Why haven't you passed out by now? said Joseph in a mock-exasperated tone. I haven't anything else; you've cleaned me out.

– Let me tell you a story, Mickey said. A true story – about myself, what's more. I lived in Germany as a child – my father was stationed there with the British army. Somehow, I ended up in a children's choir that went around the hospitals at Christmas, singing carols to the patients. On one occasion, we sang 'Silent Night' outside a patient's room – I didn't know at the time why we didn't go inside to sing to him – and a nurse came out when we finished and told us that Herr Rudolf Hess had enjoyed our singing, and thanked us very much.

– It's a good anecdote, said Joseph. Any reason for telling it to me?

– Oh, I don't know. I suppose it's got *something* to do with innocence.

– Well, look, he continued. The boys I like are young enough to inspire an idea of innocence – and it's the idea I'm interested in. Sex and innocence make a beautiful combination. But the innocence is only a question of an image – a fleeting image, an elusive image, if you like.

– I need, he said, that contradiction of innocent beauty and sex. What else would allow me to escape....

– Escape? asked Joseph.

– From everything that's routine and banal – and Mickey waved his arms expansively, as if to show how prevalent the routine and the banal really were.

– But, he went on, what sort of places do you think I have to try and find innocence in? I've sometimes imagined myself as I was when I was a kid. What would I say to myself? The child I was would be disgusted by the idea of my hanging around public toilets. And the clubs attract some dangerous characters. There've been a series of stranglings recently....

– Mickey, said Joseph, we'll have to continue this another time. I need to sleep now.

Joseph fetched blankets from the bedroom, and arranged them on the couch for his guest.

•

In the morning Joseph found that Mickey had left without waiting to say goodbye. A note had been placed on his desk:

Dear Max,

Thanks for the interesting night. So that's what they mean when they say "doing it to Webern". Crazy. You are a bit too rough, though. Be careful next time.

See you around the lindens,

Heinz.

It was an impudent joke, but it nevertheless amused Joseph. He laughed as he screwed the paper into a little ball.

Chapter Five

– Tell me, Joseph said, about the woman who became your teacher.

– When I was a child, Catherine said, I thought I was like the other children I knew, and that I'd grow to be like the adults. I was taught that I belonged to a society, a country and a history, because of accidents of time and place; and I was made to feel that I was part of nature – a physical organism amongst other organisms. I might have merged entirely with those dreams. But I was always uneasy about the way people expected me to be: my parents; my teachers; other children; and then later, my fellow students.

Catherine continued:

– She found me sitting in a cafeteria, having tea; she sat down opposite me and began to talk – and the things she said were exactly what I'd needed all my life to hear.

– Who, I thought, could she be? For I was marvelling at how much her words had affected me. She smiled, and said: I came here for one reason only: to talk to you.

– With her help, I left off being the person I thought I was; I began to retrieve myself from all the moments of my past in which I'd lost myself. It was like a building – an invisible building; you go over it in all its details so thoroughly that you can then trace through it the real lines of your spirit.

– And she left you, Joseph said.

— Well, yes — Catherine looked directly at him — yes, she went away.

— But the letters, she said. She sent me letters that dazed me with her love.

•

Side by side on the wall were two large black-and-white photographs of Botticelli's *Abundance*. Shepherdess of children, who retires into her own resplendence. Plenitude animates the lithe, graceful figure as an air or ghost. One photograph reproduced the drawing as black and grey lines, with white highlights, on an off-white ground; the other, a negative print, reversed the black to white, the white to black.

Joseph sat opposite these panels; Maeve lounged on a couch beneath them, with her legs pulled up and her head tilted back. Joseph sipped at the cognac she had brought him. He said: I dreamt last night that I was walking in a desolate field of volcanic ash, and I came to a chair, standing by itself in that field. Then I heard a voice — someone singing — and in the distance I saw Catherine. There was a pathway of white stones, through the field of ash, and she was doing a soft-shoe routine on the stones while singing a song. I could only make out the words of one line: "It's got to be a moral story...."

He fell silent. Maeve said: Is that all? — Yes, said Joseph. He took a sip of his cognac.

Maeve drew the hair away from her brow in a sudden gesture with both hands; the unexpectedly bared forehead lengthened her face in a way that startled him.

— The thing I like about your dream, she said, is that Catherine was moved to dance.

— By the way, she continued, I once knew a Jesuit cardinal who was utterly *obsessed* with dancing. He was asked to appear in a television film about tap-dancing: it was the high-point of his life.

Joseph had in fact lied: he'd withheld the last part of his dream.

He had tried to run to Catherine, but his legs were stiff with arthritis; he could only hobble, painfully. When he was no more than half way towards her, he suddenly found himself confronted by Catherine's colleague from the library.

– She's ruining herself, he said to Joseph. His voice was shrill, petulant. – She squanders herself on people who aren't worthy of her. I've watched her – I know! The man grabbed Joseph's arm.

– I don't want to hear this, Joseph said.

As Joseph shook himself free, the man blurted out:

– And then there was you! Don't worry – I followed the pair of you – more than once! I *know* what's been going on between you!

And at that point Joseph had awoken.

•

When he left Maeve's, the sun was shining on a cherry-blossom tree at the front of her house. Each cluster of blossom was fused into a lucent ring or halo surrounding a darker centre.

Catherine would take no interest in such a sight, Joseph knew; the thought moved him. Neither blossom – nor eyes.... (Maeve, on the other hand, was particularly drawn to people's eyes. Portraits, for her, were always portraits of eyes.)

Oh Catherine, he thought, a line may lead from known threshold through unknown night. And there, in the night, visible beauty gives its place to invisible beauty.

She had his hand (he felt the touch, always). No matter, then, if the way was irrevocable, on which she took him to dwell in darkness.

Biography

Ran Thomas was totally at a loss to know how to go about cheering up a bereaved woman; but he shyly edged his way across to her. Someone at the service had said to him: She's just lost her husband; do go over and speak to her – you can tell her you're from her own country.

Mercifully, she took the initiative and said, Isn't it lovely to see the fountains and all the lights from here? For they were standing on the steps of the church, looking out towards the square. Sorrow had, so to speak, veiled and attenuated the woman; and the paleness of ash-blond hair, fair skin and light-blue eyes folded into the aged, faded appearance her countenance had borrowed.

Ran thought, Lost things are supposed to be found at this time; and remembered another bleak Christmas eve, when loneliness and boredom had taken him to a meeting at the Melbourne Theosophical Society. The talk that evening had been about astral projection – a subject for which Ran could gather no enthusiasm at all. But before the speaker had taken the floor, a chubby young baritone in a dress suit, accompanied by a large, middle-aged and frumpish woman pianist, had rendered three carol-songs, preceded by the baritone's instruction to his partner: Hit it, Maudie. That detail, at least, had delighted him. On the way out of the building, Ran glimpsed (or so he thought) his ex-wife, Celia; she vanished in the next moment, and he realised it had been a hallucination. He had walked down the street to the public square, where there was a large Christmas tree; the electric lights of the tree flickered in a pattern that was reflected in the glass of the building behind it – an artificial snowfall bright like highly polished bronze. Scattered groups of people stood around the square, talking.

Now, he wished the woman a good Christmas, and went down the steps to the street, nodding to one or two others who had been at the service. There was a crowd around the fountains, and Ran, who was fascinated by the sight of jets of water, strolled over towards them, thinking: cool flames of ablution.

•

Ran's dreams had pursued him with torment. In particular, he'd suffered a recurring dream, in which he found himself wandering in a place of infinite sorrow and weariness: he knew this was hell. A companion said to him as they entered a room, He's here too, you know. A man stood with his back to them at the other end of the room; when Ran's companion had said these words, the man turned to face them and Ran recognised him: it was Christ. At this point Ran sometimes screamed, and woke to hear himself screaming as he sat upright in his bed in the darkness.

Then one night he'd dreamt that he was lost in a large, lucent city, where the houses resembled white-painted ships; and he'd looked forward to his departure as some form of release more deeply from that night on.

•

On the way to England, Ran took to spending so much time looking over the side of the ship that the ocean came to seem, for short periods, like the dreamless spaces of sleep; which were interrupted by dream encounters with other passengers and by the dream-places at which the ship stopped. At other times, the sea appeared to him as an oneiric source, submerging him in reveries.

When he had hallucinated Celia's face into a crowd outside the Theosophical Society, a brief look at pleasure at seeing him, totally improbable at that point in time as he well enough knew, flashed across her features before the image vanished. The sea also brought him phantoms of Celia that similarly appeared alive for a brief time; but it was the Celia of memory, stretching her naked body over him in bed as she blew out the candle on the table, or resting her head on his shoulder as they sat together on their livingroom floor.

And at night, Ran had often dreamt of snow, or of heavy, blinding sheets of rain, falling into the sea....

•

What had he said to the woman on the church steps? Little, or nothing. He hadn't said, Yes, I've lost my wife, too – but not through death; he hadn't said anything remotely like that.

Every picture of Celia he'd attempted had failed; after she'd left him, he tried painting over two large photographs of her, substituting his own view for that of the camera. The paint grew thicker and the strokes more violent, covering the delicate lines of her face, the shoulder-length brown hair, the vulnerable yet slightly haughty look of the eyes and mouth; and Ran quickly found that he was obliterating an image of her rather than revealing a different image: the viciousness became sadly evident.

•

Now he had virtually lost interest in painting. He kept on, a little at least; but he saw that the paintings had become schematic in such a way that they were mere illustrations of pictorial ideas. Nothing revealed itself in the painting activity itself, everything came from a given repertory; and Ran watched in vain for something new and living to emerge.

Since coming to London he'd found work as an assistant curator in an art museum; the work left him so lethargic in the evenings, that only at weekends could he gather to some focus what impulses for painting still remained.

He gave up his use of acrylic paint to concentrate on large ink-paintings – black, on long white or cream paper-scrolls – but the swiftness of execution which Ran counted upon for some increase in spontaneity, was offset by an increase in the schematised *form* of his images.

In the past, Ran had mainly worked on long horizontal panels of wood, divided vertically into extensive areas of white (or occasionally black) juxtaposed with much smaller areas which appeared as if collaged into the white or black length. These areas contained imagery of various sorts – basic still life or landscape motifs and human likenesses – simplified in form, and painted in muted colours, lighter when he used white for the void areas, darker when he used black. The juxtapositions of imagery were, in Ran's best work, emotionally allusive while visually direct. At the point where the images were held in some sort of tension, and the areas of void space and the images reinforced each other rather than detracting, he felt the painting had succeeded.

•

In the morning, on the way to work, Ran would often pass a tall and frail-looking young woman, walking slowly with the aid of a stick; her hair long and blond and hanging in curling strands. He thought (whether correctly or not) that she had some form of blood-disease.

One morning he saw her coatless and bareheaded in the rain, and thought, yes, that is how she is.

He found himself looking out for her; sometimes stopping to wonder why she had so taken hold of his mind. Chance had brought her into the proximity of death; yet in the face of this she was *stubbornly beautiful* – not, he thought, in the sense that she was possessed by mere wilfulness, nor any desperate clinging, but rather that in her countenance there was a firmness, a resistance integral to whatever was refulgent and vital in her being. That appeared basic to him; but beyond it, he didn't pretend to know how she felt; and he couldn't bring himself to speak to her. Sometimes he would see her unexpectedly in the street, as he turned a corner, and it always had the effect of a shock; in the way that the sight of someone you love, or a powerful work of art, or anything epiphanic, may jolt and disrupt your state of being. Her affliction drew his compassion; her beauty drew his admiration; and the two things fused into this intense and painful emotion that could make him recoil, as if he had been struck.

•

Ran had been inspired in his painting by the work of an older Australian artist, Bob Hall. Hall had lived for many years as an expatriate in Greece, but he continued to send his paintings to exhibitions in his native country, so that over the years Ran built up an extensive knowledge, as well as a profound love, of Hall's work.

Bob Hall's paintings each consisted of a rectangular field of pure white broken by a series of rectilinear strips, parallel to one or another of the framing edges; these strips never numbered less than three, nor more than five, and were of unequal length and width; they extended from the edges of the painting to various points across its surface, but seldom to an opposite edge. The strips were filled with abstract linear motifs, irregular and yet definite in shape, related to each other through variation or contrast. Bob Hall gave the paintings an enamel-like finish, and for the strips he employed brilliant colours orchestrated through the composition in a lucid if complex way.

Hall's involvement with form and void, pattern and non-pattern, colour and blankness, was deeply suggestive to Ran. In the way that these opposing elements equalled one another compositionally, there was an intimation of the mystical *coincidence of opposites*; and the almost Byzantine brilliance and richness of Hall's colours seemed to support a spiritual interpretation of his work.

Ran wanted his own paintings to disclose an extra-mundane order of experience. He felt no need, however, to banish the things of the senses – for his part, the spiritual could be disclosed through them.

Bob Hall remained the painter Ran most respected. He knew that Hall lived on the island of Kalymnos, and had often thought of writing to him. In fact he drafted out a number of letters, trying to express his own ambitions and frustrations as an artist, as well as his love for Hall's work. None of these ever satisfied him; and therefore were never sent. The desire to communicate with Bob Hall stayed with him, but he eventually ceased even attempting to write him a letter.

•

He copied into a notebook the words: "The blind spirit rises towards the truth by way of what is material, and seeing the light, it is resuscitated from its former submersion"; adding his own comment: "And what speaks through persons – in their entire being – enlightens me."

Shortly after Ran recorded the remark he stopped painting altogether. This was some months before his thirty-second birthday.

•

At this time, Ran began to notice a young woman who worked in another department of the museum. A tall, slender woman in her mid-twenties, with platinum-blond hair, Ran thought her beautiful, and was flattered when she showed an interest in him. Following the break-up of his marriage, Ran's emotional life had become complicated by an inability to focus his sexual feelings. Even now, it was difficult for him to do more than give way to a growing – yet still somehow vague – fascination with this woman. Her name was Emily; Ran liked its shortened form – Emmy – because it sounded agreeably old-fashioned.

One evening they went out for a drink together; and soon afterwards, it became a matter of course for them to spend considerable time in each other's company. Emmy would begin her drinking with one or two liqueurs, switch to wine, and then to whisky (which she drank mixed with lemonade). Ran matched her, drink for drink. During their first evening together, she told him that light-bulbs sometimes shattered in her presence; Ran was sceptical of this, but admitted he would enjoy *seeing* it. Just then Emily's glass shot off the table, without any apparent cause, and shattered on the floor.

•

The shower of wheat had frozen into the grey and white impression of the photograph, only to turn yellowish-brown (with the rest of the image) in time with the years of Ran's youth and manhood.

Ran and Emily sat together in his small flat. He handed Emmy the photograph, clipped (strangely enough) from a newspaper; it showed Ran's mother feeding wheat from a burlap sack to a stray flock of pigeons. She was younger then than the earliest of his memories of her; but that was his memory's fault, and he often felt that almost all of his early life had fallen away from him as the side of a mountain in a landslide.

•

Several months later, Ran looked at his features in the bathroom mirror one night as he washed, and saw that the large, solemn eyes people often remarked upon showed themselves set, as if fit only for staring uneasily. Indeed, the entire face, which Ran knew was at best *pleasant* rather than handsome, seemed fixed in an expression of unease. He passed a hand over one cheek, then slapped it, hard, with the same hand, in a release of pent-up feeling.

The night before, he had walked down a deserted and dark street in his neighbourhood, the stones thick with mud and trodden leaves; and felt that some hurt was close at hand, already bruising the air around him. Walking through into that hurt, he found himself again, sickened and frightened, at Celia's parents' house. This was after their separation: she was staying there for want of anywhere of her own to live; and Ran had turned up one evening on an impulse. Her father had refused to let him in, so he stayed out in the garden…. People coming to the door (there was presumably a dinner-party) looked at him strangely as they passed. Still he stayed, waiting for nothing; the night cold, and a light rain falling. Waiting, for the image to settle: "snow's" drift in a child's glass dome, shaken for it to rise into motion (the motion of falling). Celia's face, the last time he'd seen her, gone into sorrow, lips moving stiffly to speak, the words without flow.

Now he felt sure that there was a reason for having undergone the experience again, and that this was to do with Emily. Emmy was closely related in Ran's mind to Celia; he found himself reliving his early relationship with Celia through his meetings with Emmy. Yet Celia and Emmy were only alike in being insecure and beautiful young women who suited Ran's need – which was for an image of inviolability. Ran wanted them to inhabit a purified space, as the images in his paintings were purified of non-essential features.

Anything *mundane* appalled Celia, when it converged with her experience of love; the details of day-to-day living-together caused only frustration and eventually despair. She and Ran endured months of bitter argument. On the day that she finally moved out of their flat, Ran took her to the station to say goodbye; it was snowing lightly, and Celia wore a fur coat with the collar pulled up to just below her mouth; he kissed her lips, and their coldness stayed fixed in his mind afterwards, for it was his last physical contact with her.

Ran began to realise that seeing Emily through his memories of Celia, he failed to bring her into focus as an individual. But he saw there was also an ambiguity in Emily's being. She spoke a great deal of the importance for her of faithfulness, which was not a mere attitude or mode of behaviour towards another person, but rather conformity to an ideal state of being that in some sense included her relationship to the person she loved. However, she saw no connection between faithfulness and the sexual act, regarding sex as a matter of ethical indifference. Emmy was, in fact, promiscuous, and Ran felt disturbed and confused that she should so freely sleep with other men.

So as love had grown between Ran and Emily, discord had also developed, and these two were soon hopelessly intertwined. A particularly violent argument had occurred in the past week, ending with Ran walking away from Emmy and Emmy following and shouting at him in the street.

Now Ran left the bathroom and entered his darkened living-room; he didn't turn the light on, but found his way across the room to the window, and gazed out into the night. A few plant-pots and a small white enamel bowl stood on a ledge, the bowl distinct yet ghostly by dint of its colour and by the sound of the thin rain striking it.

•

The following day, Ran arranged for two weeks' leave from his job, and booked a flight to Greece.

•

Ran thought: the eye feels for the assent of stone, plaster and wood, as much as grass or flowers....

In the suburbs of Athens, he walked a street that led to an intersection where he encountered the large, block-like houses typical of his childhood walks; old, plaster-faced buildings, with blue or cream or yellow-ochre paintwork that had darkened with age.

He caught a train to Piraeus, wandering the crowded streets for an hour – until it was time for the boat to Kalymnos.

•

His attention was drawn from the clusters of houses along the hill back to the expanse of the sea, and then to a solitary figure on the hill, or a herd of goats (their bells jangling in the distance), before the sea claimed his attention once more. The light was intense; scintillations seemed to etch or burn themselves into the space of his vision.

Amongst some scattered debris in the blue water, Ran's eye picked out bright fragments – pieces of red-painted wood struck by the light; and he remembered a red-flowered tree against a deep blue sky – the images both like and unlike each other.

Ran had spent the earlier part of the day trying to find Bob Hall. A taxi-driver had located Hall's house for him, after a number of enquiries, but Hall was not there. So Ran went to a café for lunch, and then took a walk around the island, ending up at this point near the quay. He thought: I'll wait here for another half-hour, and then go back to his house;

but at that moment he noticed, a short distance away, a man
walking along – a tall and lean man of late middle age, with
a thin face and a mass of curly grey hair. Ran recognised him
from a photograph he'd once seen of Bob Hall.

He began to walk towards the man, who saw him and
stopped, calling out to Ran: Are you looking for me?

– Yes, said Ran.

Round About Midnight

She had lived through successive levels of degradation, successive bodies of truth, until she'd ended as a prostitute. Or so, at any rate, Simon explained it to her.

•

– Remember, said Leon, you could always write a story about it. He beamed at me good-naturedly.

– No, I don't write stories any more, I said.

– Well, he said, the funny thing is, you seemed to get along with her just fine.

She had been sitting with a girlfriend in the small, predominantly Black pub; they were just about the only white people in the place, at least until Leon and his friends and I arrived.

Leon and the others were already drunk by the time we got to the pub, and in the mood to be mischievous.

There was a small combo squeezed into a corner of the room: trumpet, tenor sax, electric guitar, string bass and drums. They weren't especially good, but when they played an old tune – whether it was *Pound Cake* or *Destination Moon* – they played with feeling, and with enough sophistication for the tunes to sound right. The people in the bar certainly liked them. – Oh beautiful, one Black guy exclaimed after they'd played *I Cover the Waterfront*.

Leon and his friends tried to engage the two girls in conversation, while at the same time pulling me more and more into the situation, manoeuvring things, to my embarrassment, to the point where I was being thrust at the one young woman, Helen. For her part, she seemed more amused than anything else.

Then when we were about to leave, she did something unexpected. As I was going out the door, she thrust a piece of paper into my hand. Although I'd not at all been prepared for this, it was not necessary for me to look at the paper to know what was written on it.

•

I had almost forgotten about Helen, when one afternoon I was standing on a railway platform and, just as the train pulled in, I noticed that she had been standing beside me. We looked at each other, both rather shyly. It seemed a matter of course to sit together in the carriage. And talk.

•

– Writing stories, I said, is rather like acting. It's an involvement in an unreal world. A shadow life. And that is dangerous.

Leon at one time had made abstract drawings and collages in which he sought to make the few marks or pasted elements establish or frame the predominant emptiness, void, of the white paper. Later he had worked on a critical biography of the metaphysician René Guénon. Leon survived – as I did – through all sorts of employment and unemployment: bookselling, dishwashing, labouring, baby-sitting, dole money.

One afternoon we'd gone to a market together to do

some shopping. Leon had bought a pumpkin to make some soup, and it shared his carrier bag with a bottle of wine and a volume of Plato. Leon told me of a plan he had to set up a nursery, which he intended to run more-or-less single-handedly. The main problem was that in order to obtain a licence, there had to be a qualified nurse on the staff. However, he'd thought of a way around this. He knew a junkie nurse who had stopped going out to work and now sat at home shooting up. He could pay her a little money to be nominally involved, just to make the set-up seem respectable.

With some people, it was as if they desired, in a special sense, to be "nothing" and "no one", and yet couldn't help achieving some distinction, in spite of themselves. That was the way I often thought of Leon. Imagine a man who retires from the world, becoming a hermit. Over the years he writes poems to mark the course of his days. One day he meets a stranger and gives him the poems. The stranger eventually gets them published; and in this way the hermit in time finds himself with some sort of reputation in the world, against his inclination and will.

A photograph of Leon, in which he sits, in a sunny place, on the ground; with his two young children – boy and girl – sitting beside him. He's dressed in a rough open shirt, with the sleeves rolled up, and brown corduroy trousers. He is smiling good-naturedly; his head is bald on top but at the back the brown hair is long and wind-blown and he has a long, thick beard. The two children are naked.

•

Simon could be found at one of a number of pavement cafés in the city. Those who knew him well, or those who paid well enough, would also be able to see him in his flat. Most of these people were his disciples.

He taught that truth – and spirituality – lay in the unconditional exercise, the pure play, of the will. However, "ordinary" people had no will to speak of; they were so conditioned that they were as good as automata, and their actions had no claim to being "theirs" at all.

•

I had arranged to meet Helen at a café in the city centre. When I arrived there I found her already seated with a man. Somehow, the thought crossed my mind that she had picked him up. But I didn't want to think that, for more than one reason. So I decided he was simply a friend; and I went over and sat down with them. She introduced him as Simon.

The conversation dragged badly on that occasion, and I left after a short time. However, Simon invited me to meet him and Helen in his flat the next day.

That night I had a dream (and I should say that I dream rarely). I was a small boy again, and I stood in the middle of a street. I could hear my father calling me from a little distance away. Between us there was a huge pile of shit, about the size of two cars stacked one on another. Nothing *living* had produced that, I thought, and was afraid. My father was trying to induce me to walk across to him. He became irritated and yelled at me, For hell's sake, you can always go *around* it, you know!

As I continued to stand there, staring at it, he called to me more gently, Well, I only meant you don't have to go *through* it.

•

The next day when I saw Helen and Simon, Simon admitted that he had read one of my stories.

I was about to say I no longer wrote stories, but decided to skip it.

It was at this meeting that I began to find that I disliked Simon. He said he wanted to show me a passage in a book Helen had been reading, which he found extremely amusing.

He read it out:

"Separated from the person he loved, not by class, but by age and an old scandal, his vision of the 'Guild of St. George', the society where there was to be no rich, no poor, no steam-engines, only a pleasant and useful agricultural life, was quite clearly determined by the notion that this was the only environment in which he, a fifty-year-old divorced man, could live in untroubled happiness with a child of twelve."

– People are so *weak*, he concluded.

I quoted Simone Weil to him, that the Christian revolution consisted in not despising the weak for their weaknesses.

He laughed uproariously at that.

•

A white-painted room, the white discoloured and scratched. Heavy green curtains. Prints on the walls: Bosch's *Garden of Earthly Delights*, with its monstrous *Hell* panel; a little painting of Dante and Beatrice meeting in a tiny garden, painted simply, almost naively, with an innocent wonder in the faces, and the gazes which meet.

A large blue-green-feathered bird with a small head and gnarled beak stood on a shelf, with an earthenware jug next to it. On another shelf, some large green pieces of fruit (I do not know their name), one of them with a segment taken out so that the fruit showed its dark brown kernel. Near them, a glass jug, half full of water.

Oh, your large eyes, Helen, your large, serious, beautiful eyes.

•

– There are encounters that seem innocent enough, but you keep wanting to see the person again, and if at the beginning to see them *at all* is so much a thing as scarcely to be hoped for, eventually you want more and more, as if nothing satisfies you. And yet if you tried to just recall that person's features very precisely, you might not be able to do even that: only a vague image would appear, or a series of features, not all together but one by one, without any hope of piecing them together properly.

Her lips were parted, and as I said these things, I thought strangely of how I would like to run my tongue over her white teeth.

– You might, I said, even feel obliged to go on seeing a person purely because you can't otherwise remember what they look like.

I realised how stupid the whole line of thought was. She continued to just look at me.

– Have you ever noticed, I said, how dissipation and illness can mark a person, physically, in much the same way – so that you mightn't know at first which was the cause?

– Am I making sense? I said. My forehead was beaded.

– Why are you making yourself ill? she said, taking my hand; her eyes gathered a sorrowing aspect.

– I feel haunted by the way someone… *disappears*, by presenting herself in an image which, changing to a contradictory or divergent image, vanishes. For you, there was a block of time during which you spoke and acted in a way that wouldn't remain, not even appearing in memory a few hours later, when the effects of the alcohol had worn off. That was fairly obvious even by the time I saw you in the hospital ward. Apart from your memory, this area, a disjunctive area of time, was itself marked by a series of changes: different images of yourself, alternating or metamorphosing. I know this is so obvious it may seem banal. After all, it's an exaggeration of a process going on with all of us all of the time. It's part of what the Buddhists mean, when they say the self is impermanent, in the sense of being in a state of flux….

It came into my mind how it was also said that the *Skandhas* regroup to form another life, but I stopped speaking, as I saw she wanted to say something.

Quiet and harsh. – Is supernatural. Of necessity.

•

We had gone to a party at a place owned by one of Helen's acquaintances. The party was something of a washout, and as there was little else to do, we concentrated on drinking wine. Helen got drunk fairly quickly. And whereas normally she tends to be rather closed-in, private, she became effusive, sometimes flamboyant. She veered from spitting wine at an unfortunate young man who was trying to talk to us about Hermann Hesse, to telling me, very sadly, about her cousin, who had been her first boyfriend and who had hanged himself from a stair-rail. She said she had loved him "absolutely" – stressing the word – repeating it – so that I might know something of what she felt. (Helen also told me later that he had said, shortly before he died, that he hated her.) I'm not sure how long ago this had been – maybe eight years – but she was (not surprisingly) obsessed by it all. As her drinking was getting out of hand, I suggested we both leave, and she smilingly agreed. We walked down to her bus stop, and I asked about a tendency she had at times to be cool with me: was it, I said, out of some dislike? But she said it was due to her being afraid of other people. At the bus stop she didn't want to take either of the buses that went past. She asked me (pathetically, as such a question must be) if she was crazy – asked me several times, and I said no each time. Taking my hand, she pulled me over to a seat near the bus stop, and dug her head into my shoulder so that I was conscious of how hard her skull felt. Although she had said before that she was not a "physical sort of person", she now asked if I'd take her home to bed with me.

Then only half an hour, perhaps, until I would begin my vigil, waiting in the casualty department, waiting for two hours until they released her, waiting while people with knife- or broken-glass-wounds came through, dripping blood on the floor….

It was around midnight. With a couple of other people, I helped to hold her down; apart from a bad cut on the palm of her hand, she hadn't been physically injured, but she was having convulsions, and seemed only semiconscious (although the ambulance-woman, when I asked her, said she was in fact conscious and was, even in such a grave situation, acting out a part). Two policemen had arrived first – one of them asking me, Is she *always* like this? – and then a little later the ambulance; one of the cops and I drove to the hospital with her.

I had to tell them how she had become more and more depressed – and progressively less controllable in her moods and actions. We caught a train, but only two stops down the line she rushed out of the carriage before I could stop her, the doors immediately closing behind her. However, the train remained in the station, and after a while the doors opened again; I left the carriage, and my fears leapt up when I saw a group of people lifting something from the tracks. As I got closer the "something" was definitely a body and although I knew who it must be I didn't want to admit to myself that it was Helen, until I was too close not to recognise her.

When I saw Helen again at the hospital, just prior to her being discharged, she was both bitter and petulant, saying over and over again that "next time" she *would* kill herself, that she was "not made for life", and so on, and on….

•

– You know that she hates you, he said. Or *don't* you know? She's quite vehement about it.

– Yes, I know, I said. (For what was I to suppose? I had walked over to her place one day, with the ground covered in ice – the ice was so dangerous that a friend of mine had slipped the previous day, skinning part of her face, breaking a tooth and splitting her top lip – but Helen had refused to let me in. When I asked her why, I received only hysterical abuse.) However, I had no desire to hear about it from Simon. I had come to regard him as someone I wished to have nothing to do with. And yet I was sitting with him in a café.

– Can you guess what we did together last night? he asked.

– Maybe you watched TV, I said.

– No, *no*, he said, you really disappoint me. *No* imagination.

– Maybe.

– No, really, he repeated, you're *so* unimaginative… you write stories, but you have no imagination.

– I *used* to write stories, I said; I've stopped. But let's skip it.

– No, he said, we didn't watch TV. I shat into a pan, and Helen got undressed; I smeared her with shit, all over her body.

His eyes watched me for any sign of emotion.

– So? I said. What's that to me?

– I thought you'd be interested, Simon went on. He paused, and then said: Aren't you going to ask me if she enjoyed it?

– No, I said, I'm not.

– Well, I'll tell you anyway.

– Like hell you will! I shouted, until that moment unaware of just how angry I was becoming with him.

– Oh, you're so *sensitive*….

I stood up from the table and in the same instant lashed out at his face with my open hand; then I turned and walked out of the café. About two blocks away I looked back, but there was no one following.

•

– You mean the woman we met in the pub that night? Leon asked.

– Yes, I said.

– Well, he said, she seemed nice enough. Are you involved with her in some way?

– Yes; but there's this guy she hangs around with, named Simon….

– Her boyfriend?

– No, she told me he's not her boyfriend. They sleep together, but they don't fuck.

Leon raised his eyebrows. – So he's not her boyfriend.... Just what is it you're trying to say?

– He's... you could say he's a magician, I said. In the way that Gurdjieff was: he preaches spiritual realisation, and has a flock of followers – and with the pretence of developing their will, he exercises a not-so-sublime hegemony over them. And Helen – I guess Helen, too....

– You mean she's in his power, too? He thought, and then said: Or part of his power?

– I'm not sure, I said. Anyway, the other night I had a fight with him – sort-of. I struck him.

– Don't tell me any more, said Leon.

– Why?

– Because you should flee them like the devil.

Voice and Name

Each had been sent to protect me.

The vampire leaned close, breath cold and fetid on my neck, spoke words of comfort. Reaching out a hand to gingerly touch the hem of my coat, drawing his lips back in a smile. I let my head remain high though in heart it sunk on my chest; not wanting, either, that he be *too* familiar, I drew away a little.

We stood in the street in rain.

It was late evening, and the others grouped round me now, to show concern. O God, I thought; O my God; and remembered then how once a man trying to befriend me took me in his car to a pub where friends of his were gathered.

He told me as we drove of a nervous breakdown he'd suffered; and then of the problems of his friends, some of them spastics, some of them with speech defects. I was in sorrow; none of what he told me did any more than deepen that sorrow which sped toward the pub where his friends were drinking and drinking: a park in night and wind and in wind and a little light the faces, chimeric, caught and warped. One of them, a woman, decided upon me; although I could do little to answer, she kept trying to engage me and, smiling, revealed teeth black with dirt.

But obviously there is meant nothing here by way of *comparison*. The ghost with his wide eyes and his mouth perpetually open, the lips near-colourless; something in his inchoate rasping, panting sounds suggested sympathy. And the man-eater, face so terrible, jaws so large – yet: yet still: his averted look gave me to understand that he knew how hideous I must think him. Yet he, too, had been given to protect me.

•

Hōnen and I stood looking at a row of paintings with chalk-markings, like corrections, over the paint. The artist, Shōhōbō, had once made a portrait of Hōnen, which Hōnen corrected with lines in chalk. After that, Shōhōbō always incorporated such marks in his paintings.

•

A telephone call, to go to a neighbour's (a prostitute) to tell her that her youngest child had been taken to hospital after an epileptic fit; waiting then, in the uncarpeted room, speaking then, with the room smelling of dog piss and the woman, strongly, of drink.

As I walked back out into the night street and crossed the road, I noticed that the vampire had been standing in the shadows at a house on the corner; his eyes following.

•

At last I received a letter, warm and friendly, from her; suggesting we meet the following week. That evening I caught a bus to go and visit a friend. During the journey two girls got on the bus and sat down in front of me. One of them looked very much like the girl who had written – and yet wasn't *this* girl younger? And weren't her clothes quite unlike the sort of clothes the other girl wore (or at least that I knew her to wear)? But why couldn't I decide for sure? I kept looking at her, trying to make up my mind. Then the bus arrived at my stop and as I got up to leave, her friend looked directly at me. Later when I saw the girl I knew, I told her of this incident and asked, Was it you? – No, she laughed; then she said, Why did you stare like that? I could feel your eyes on me.

In imagination: sitting in a public square, with fountains, pigeons, a stream of people. Of each passer-by she asked me, What would you think of that one? Would you want to know him? Does she attract you?

Black railings patterned with rust and with splotches and threads of light blue paint. Steps, stone, down to basement dwellings. Rotten leaves, papers, other trash on steps or beside, unremoved.

•

Hōnen nodded approvingly. We were in a café, drinking tea. The vampire and the others sat at another table, back from ours. I noticed the man-eater looked even more ferocious, and yet even more sorrowful.

Hōnen said, If you should find a man longing for the Land of Perfect Bliss, and calling on the sacred name, even if he were to be a denizen of a world far removed from this one of ours, think of him with no less compassion than that of a father or mother. He added: Lend your aid to those who are poor in the necessaries of life. I asked Hōnen about the writing of poetry, which he knew engaged me greatly. – It is not necessarily wrong, he replied. It may indeed become a sin to a man, or it may prove meritorious. I mentioned his own poems, quoting lines and phrases that had particularly reached me: "heart its colouring gains"; "the hour of that day come"; "the voice of him who calls His name". We spoke then of "the purple colour of attaining". I told him that heedless of society's dictates I wished nothing more than to help everyone I came across, regardless of their position or background, while living in poverty and regarded as a complete fool by all. – That is all very well, said Hōnen, but one ought not to drink. – Although, he added, it is the way of the world.

•

I couldn't bear the sound of their voices any longer.

Having taken refuge in the room upstairs, the voices of the girl and her friends, the couple we were staying with and their other guest, penetrated that refuge and gave me no peace.

She had been questioning me, earlier, about the origin of my depression. What could I have said? I didn't even say that I loved her; the difference in our ages, and my friendship with her parents, had always been against it.

The other voices thronged around her, and she sat in the middle of them.

Where was I, anyway? I was where I could only sit in a distance, while those voices drove me wild. Voices and not *the voice*. Voices of social conformity, voices of those who had benefitted materially from that conformity, voices of petti-ness and lust, not love, not constancy or faith; voices of the world, and I outside, joined to ghostliness.

•

Leaving the house, more and more estranged, aware that I was being rude to those people, I walked down the country road, the night air crisp, the stars clear. The road was largely unlit, and I had often to stand to one side while a car passed. I came to a crossroads, and wondering which fork to take, it occurred to me that someone else was there. I held my head high, though in heart it rested on my chest, in despair. He didn't say anything. As he came closer, my eyes made out clearly the thin, pale lips and wide eyes. But I had known it was him even before he drew close enough for me to see him properly. – Are you going back? another spoke, from behind. It was the vampire's voice. – It must be cold... for you, he said. I turned and looked at him. I was beginning to cry. The only direction available was that leading back to the house, and I took it.

•

Precise red leaves. Stones. Blue flame. Window.

In the morning: through the morning: and into the afternoon: sparrows come into the kitchen through the window; noise of wings, of feet scrabbling on surfaces (table, floor).

•

Reaching the garden we sat down on a mound while the others went into the house to prepare lunch. I tried to shield my face with my hand, because of tears, not copious, but tears just the same.

Two people: walking in a field, looking for a path in vain, then taking the main road a long way.

•

And even now to dwell on that break, that gap in time. I stayed once in her parents' flat, while the family was away on holiday. She was sixteen, and isolated inside her own tenderness. She seemed impressed by me, as an older person, drawn to me, too; and this warmed me at the same time as I found it appalling. Looking at any of a dozen reminders of her, sundry objects in the flat that only *she* would possess, I quite simply vowed not to see her again for a year. And I didn't.

•

– What does it matter, she said....

She sat down next to me, her thigh against mine; she caressed my back as I continued to stare into the distance.

The blue field of silence washed over the words, blue water and blue sky, deepening to black.

(For Will Petersen)

Blues

There was a crashing sound, and I ran up the stairs and turned the red handle of the door; entering the room, I saw that the windowpane had been smashed. Directly below the window was a new painting, which I'd left on the floor to dry.

– What about Annabel, I had asked my mother a week before; do you still see her? – Oh, she's dead, my mother said. – But how? How did she die? – I don't know, she said.

•

Two figures run through a park at night, around a fountain and amongst the trees: hide-and-seek; hallucinatory running-speeds – and moments of stillness (they stop; laughing at each other). This could be a dream, but it is not. These figures course death in flash after flash.

•

Annabel wrote me a letter, which I could hardly understand at all; and of which I remember almost nothing: I wish I had it with

117

me now. She had become very religious at that time and had written to remind me of my own "most real nature"; that much I can remember. I can also remember a distressing incident she recounted in the letter. One night she was awoken by, she said, God's voice speaking to her. She thought she was being called to go out into the streets in search of her God, in the flesh; but when she did so, she was set upon by a couple of drunks, who tried to rape her. I can't remember any more of what the letter said.

•

As we walked down the stone steps, John told me how he had found there, once, the contents of a woman's handbag, scattered as if in a struggle. He'd discovered, amongst the rest, a letter with the address of a job, but when he enquired at that place they had not known of the woman.

In the car, the woman lay unmoving in the man's arms. A cop stood at the open window.

The sea was calm; we leaned against the iron-mesh of the barrier, and looked across the body of water to the lights on the opposite shore.

•

I had to spend the day at college carrying a travelling-case from room to room; I'd been unable to take it home before going in that morning. A fellow student, when I happened to phone him the following day, said that when I'd been observed with the case, it'd been assumed I was going away. Then I found myself attempting to speak to him about her, the woman Elspeth, and to no avail.

•

The evening before I was to leave for Australia, Elspeth telephoned me.

I remembered another time: leaning in a doorway, waiting until she had come up to where I stood. We talked there for a short while; she broke off the conversation by saying that her children would be standing in the cold at the bus-shelter where she collected them, and that if she were late they'd tell her she was a "bad mother".

When I confessed to fears about the trip to Australia, she said that was only natural: you had to expect that by the time of entering the plane everything would blur and start swimming.

•

From the prevailing darkness, a silver-green edge – of a metal tray, set on the table – shines from the doorway. I was worried about the amount of blood I was passing with my urine; if it kept up, I'd have to go back to the hospital.

•

Driving over the bridge, I looked out the window to see a flock of gulls wheeling across the sky, the darkness riding them.

On one occasion, John had caught the last ferry for the evening and found himself the only passenger aboard. He described the event as something strangely joyous, but there came to my mind Melville's dream of Edgar Poe, as a lone man standing on the deck of a half-wrecked boat at sea. A short distance from our station at the waters, there was a small stone fountain, broken and hence disused, in a lonely pond. – There's a clock without hands, not far, he said; it's disturbing. – I feel that here, I said. So we walked away.

•

I was left alone in my friend's studio, with the heavy slabs of coloured glass standing against the walls, the sketches pinned up, and paintings stacked one against another.

Dreams moving over an ocean's plenitude. Extremity, in which one waits, attendant upon what is unknown. But this is desire and love. I, hopelessly, am waiting.

•

I was probably fourteen, so she would have been about thirty-nine. She had stayed at our house overnight; much to the reluctance of my mother, who warned me not to use a particular towel, as Annabel had used it, and she was "dirty". After Annabel had left, I went upstairs by myself; standing in the empty bathroom with her image in my mind, I said: I love you.

•

It was a half an hour too early when I arrived at the station, so instead of catching a bus the rest of the distance, I decided to walk. At half-seven it was already dark, and the air was cold.

Once, I had stepped into a train-carriage, on the way to a film-show, and had found Elspeth standing there. The film included footage of ceremonial dancing by some African tribesmen, dressed in costumes made of feathers. The audience laughed at these images; their laughter annoyed me. I was reminded, strangely, of the mating-ritual of a certain water bird, which performs complex, ballet-like actions across the surface of the water, with rapid linear movements and sudden turns.

I came to the door and rang the bell; Elspeth's oldest child, a girl of thirteen, opened the door to me.

•

She was probably the gentlest person I have ever known.

(Thinking of her now, late at night, in the rain, as I wait for a taxi – remembering how she wouldn't take a black-painted taxi home from my parents', because to her black signified death.)

•

When I saw John again, at a bookshop where we had arranged by phone to meet, it was eight years since we had last seen each other. (I cannot even remember the circumstances of that last meeting. In the intervening years we had kept in touch, if intermittently, by letter.) We later went back to John's home, and it being evening by then, he went into his children's bedroom to say goodnight to them. – Daddy, said one of them, what are you doing here? – I *live* here, he said, laughing. Sitting in the living-room, drinking coffee, I noticed a large painting on the wall, which reminded me of the work of an English Pop artist, Richard Hamilton. – Who's the painter? I asked. – Oh, he's not really a painter, John said in his quiet, measured voice; he's a framer. He does some collage and some "fool-the-eye" effects, that sort of thing…. He shrugged. – People liked the first one he did, so he continued doing them, and even gets commissions now. After a pause, he added: He's a good frame-maker, though.

•

John sent me an essay by the Anglo-Sri Lankan writer Ananda Coomaraswamy; in which I found the following quotation: "When my heart beheld Love's sea, of a sudden it left me and leapt in."

•

She told me of her experience, as a child, of the darkness, the terror of dark spaces, of how it had stayed with her, and had come into the light of the present as something that she must recognise and deal with.

I had seen her many times, noticed her in the refectory at lunch (sometimes with her children), passed her in corridors and in the college library; and this for a long time.

I was sitting in a new class, when she came in, late after taking her children to school, and sat down, beside me.

The Serendipity Caper

They had exchanged portrait medallions, as a token of love; a love pursued outside of physical passion and marriage.

– Love is said by Orpheus to be without eyes because he is above the intellect, Pico explained to Giovanna.

– Uh huh, said Giovanna Tornabuoni.

But Pico della Mirandola had been speaking with his friend Marsilio, and the mystery they pursued weighed on his mind.

– Oh, said Pico, if I could go to Germany to consult the works of the late Cardinal Nicolas of Cusa.... For Leone Battista has said the esteemed Nicholas wrote many things concerning the purification of the Body of Christ, and the Antichrist's persecution of the faithful. Perhaps then we should see into this mystery more clearly!

– My poor Giovanni, she said; but added, Woe to us all in this time.

•

My friend and I sat on a station platform one rainy evening, talking about the painter Angela whom we'd just visited. She was convinced the world was to be imminently redeemed by a holocaust few would survive. Wind-flogged, buildings on fire behind them, survivors would have to find a way to cross a watery abyss: a monarch falling on his sword, in anamorph.

•

They knew well the necessity of receptiveness to the material signs and portents of occurrences in the spiritual order; they knew also that these were often chanced upon in unlikely ways, unforeseen places.

Sometimes they would each find, co-incidentally, some especial thing that gave fresh thought. – Our souls are everywhere at the same time, Marsilio would say, invoking Plotinus; we needn't wonder, then, at correspondences of the spirit! And they would continue to sort out new evidence.

Dreams came to some, giving presentiments; Marsilio would tell of his mother, who saw in a dream that her husband, Ficino the doctor, would fall from his horse, and where it would happen; and who foresaw divers other things. But their own dreams seemed to give them little illumination.

One day Giovanni Pico told his friend of how he'd dreamt he was about to enter his own house, when he saw that the startlingly obese corpse of a Black woman was being hoisted out of the top window in a sling, by means of some mechanical apparatus. – When I saw this, he said, I felt shock and pity…somehow fear, too. – Hmm, said Ficino; I don't *know* about this….

•

His tipped glass reflected gold briefly in the window; an implacable deep blue reigned outside.

But they refused to bring him any more wine. Night after night, he was there deeply drunk, if not also drugged and raving.

He pointed to the stuffed boar's-head on the wall. – The saviour, he said.

The following day, remorse and self-hatred would claim him.

•

I lay for a long time on the threshold of waking, in a state of terror and panic for which I could find no reason; and locked into that mute space, I desperately tried to make myself scream out loud and break the spell, for I didn't know how I could bear it any longer. Throughout, some trace of a presence hovered over my prostrate body; one word, a name, formed itself in my head: Trakl.

•

My friend Chris and I were talking about chance, as is Chris' wont. We were looking through his texts on design, futurology and other subjects, which utilised quoted passages drawn randomly from books apposite to his feelings about a theme; around these passages he would improvise his own thoughts. He also played me a tape-recording of the composer John Cage reading from a chance-derived text based on Thoreau's journals. As we talked and listened, various memories of our years of friendship welled up, aided by the good wine we were drinking.

When I was leaving, and Chris came out to the front of the house to say goodbye, we saw a group of his neighbours – including a Chinese concert-pianist who lived next door – standing near a tree from which the crystalline ornamentation of a nightingale's song could be heard; although the bird itself was hidden by the branches and leaves.

Together we listened to the nightingale in the tree at midnight.

•

They knew that the Beasts and the Antichrists would appear in such a way as to invert and parody the figures and stages of redemption, so that, as Joachim of Fiore had written, even the Final Judging would be travestied by the Infernal Hosts:

"And because… Christ Jesus will come openly in the glory of his majesty surrounded with a heavenly army of angels and men, so too Satan will appear openly with armies of wicked men, so that on the basis of dread of his forces he may pretend to be him who will come to judge the living and the dead and the world by fire."

Accidental details would bear the descent from which the faithful would, eventually, rise.

– Being divine, our souls can divine many things, Marsilio liked to say. The gifts of God – divination, poetry, philosophy, love – are a frenzy; which must be given back to God.

•

He wrote to a friend: "It is such an unspeakable misfortune when the world falls apart in our hands. O my God, what judgement has been visited upon me! Tell me that I must have the strength to live on and do what is right. Tell me that I am not mad. Stony darkness has come over me. O my friend, how small and wretched I have become."

Drug-addict, alcoholic, with an incestuous love for his sister and an inability to deal with the social world, Trakl wrote poems which were an easy prey for the reductionist hermeneutics of psychoanalysts, those detectives of psychic labyrinths and back-alleys.

•

His harsh and splendid friend! How he had shocked those dignitaries with their petty concern for rank and privilege, shouting to make them quake! They had offered him a Red Hat – and he had answered them, I want no hats, no mitres great or small. I only want the one You, O Lord, gave to your saints: death. A red hat, a hat of blood, that is what I want.

The City of Florence knew well how his preaching of Genesis reached the point of the Flood being visited upon a guilty humankind, co-incidentally with the French King Charles' entrance into Italy – Charles, who was God's instrument for the chastisement of the country. Pico was present when Fra Girolamo rent the air of the Church of San Marco with the words, Behold! I will bring waters upon the face of the earth. Pico's hair stood on end: for the Apocalypse was drawing on.

•

Georg Trakl staggered across the icy street; his arm thrown around the shoulders of an ageing prostitute whose love he held, without sensual passion.

His gift of poetry was turned towards the immaterial; and in that turning the materialistic culture of his time stood condemned; the rotting objects and the putrescent flesh – as he saw it – of a decaying civilisation trembled before the onslaught of redemption. – Humankind, he said, has never before sunk so deeply as it has in our generation.

•

Her children tittered and sniggered at me, with my long hair and my shy demeanour; her friends found me impossible. How odd it seems that I ever entered into that world she lived in, of an imminent holocaust; the light of which she tried to evoke in those strange relief-paintings with their crude and harsh radiance – bursting forth from the crumbling, melting, burning forms of a burning world.

We sat on a bench at the station, my friend and I, with the

rain coming down, and I was struck speechless thinking of the sadness of all earthly things.

Dream Images of Life

The samurai Jirō Naozane, because of dissatisfaction with his relations with the Shōgun, became a priest under the name Rensei and before long a disciple of Hōnen. Hōnen on their first meeting told Rensei that to attain salvation all he need do was to recite the *Nembutsu*, or sacred invocation (*Namu Amida Butsu*). Amida Buddha's Vow, he said, was to save all those who earnestly called upon his name. At this Rensei burst into uncontrollable tears. When Hōnen at length asked him why he wept so, he answered: I supposed you would tell me I should have to cut off my hands and feet and give up my life if I would be saved.... *Simplicity*: what was it? What did it mean? The two men walked down to the harbour and stood looking out over the dark calm water while one told the other of an evening when he had caught the last ferry, alone. They walked back by way of a small park where there was a broken fountain, the water still and stagnant. *Nembutsu*-followers were said to be reborn, after their death, on a lotus in a Pure Land in the West; Rensei made a vow that he wouldn't accept rebirth in the Pure Land unless it was in the highest rank of the highest class of that land. He had a dream which reassured him about this attainment: he was standing with ten others around a golden lotus flower, and he said to them: No one but myself can get up on that flower; at which he found himself sitting on top of it. Rensei was the headman of his district and if he thought any man guilty of bad conduct, he would make him carry a heavy horse-trough on his back or fetter him hand and foot.

•

Once when Hōnen went to visit the Regent Kanezane – a devout follower, of whom Hōnen was to say, We have had an affinity for each other from a former life – Rensei insisted on going along. While Hōnen spoke to the Regent, Rensei waited outside. Not being able to hear the sermon that was being delivered, Rensei exclaimed loudly: What a hatefully vile world is this anyway. Surely Paradise must be vastly different from this. Hearing his words, Kanezane had him invited inside. First one room, then another, window, window, light on a glass bowl of flowers, light on a glass bowl of fruit. Traffic outside; pavement, trees. He pared down to the core. Cool fire of light off burnished steel: the inner body was as if a mini-malist sculpture, a streamlined bird of aspiration. Rensei said, Birth into the Land of Bliss is a reward which belongs to the future, and is still far distant. And yet here I am thus quickly entering upon the enjoyment of it here and now in the pres-ent, when I am allowed to come right inside such a palace as this. Surely no one could attain the like except by the practice of the *Nembutsu*, as the Original Vow prescribed.

•

Rensei wrote of a strange dream: "...I saw a slender golden lotus with an elongated stem without any branches on it, growing out of the ground. Around it stood some ten per-sons, to whom I addressed the following words – 'No one

but myself can get up on that flower.' No sooner had I said
this than, without knowing how I did it, I found myself sitting on it, and with that I awoke." She sat back in the chair,
in the centre of the room, and lit a cigarette. Light on the
right side of her face. Dark, soft hair. Rensei said, I have had
dreams over and over again of being born into the highest
rank of the highest class. Regent Kanezane wrote to Hōnen
about the reputation Rensei was gaining because of the wonderful omens he received in his dreams: "...everything connected with this man is passing strange. I can hardly keep the
tears back at the very thought of him."

•

The samurai Jirō Naozane had distinguished himself in
battle as a warrior; but due to poor relations with the Shōgun,
Naozane became a priest under the name of Rensei. He was
advised to call on Hōnen to ask his advice on some questions
relating to the after-life. She told him of how on a weekend
in the country with some others, she'd had a fit of crying and
been comforted by another young woman. She'd been subject to such outbursts for about ten years, that is, since her
mid-teens, as if they compensated for or expressed some
emotional frustration. Or rather she said, to do with love.
More and more he wandered streets to hold nothing; eyeing
women passing by or sitting in restaurants, shops, offices.
Hōnen wrote to Rensei: "It is a terrible fact that devils always
get in the way of those who are striving for Buddhahood,
and so you want to be on your guard. This is why I call your
attention to this fact, for auspicious as these wonderful
omens must be, it is possible that evil spirits will try to take
advantage of them to lead you astray, and so you will do well
to be very circumspect, and be much in prayer to Amida."

•

Once when Hōnen went to visit the Regent Kanezane, Rensei insisted on accompanying him. While Hōnen spoke to the Regent, Rensei waited outside. Not being able to hear the words of Hōnen's sermon, Rensei exclaimed loudly, What a hatefully vile world is this anyway. Surely Paradise must be vastly different than this. He stood at the top of the stairs. At the bottom was the kitchen, in the kitchen there would be a knife. He would take the knife into the bathroom and lock the door. He felt bad about doing it in her flat, but then everything felt bad. He thought of an incident some years previous, when he'd been surprised with a knife at his wrist in the kitchen of a house he shared with several other people. He heard the door open and close again. He was still standing at the top of the stairs. Light on the right side of her face. Kanezane had Rensei brought in. Rensei said, Birth into the Land of Bliss is a reward which belongs to the future, and is still far distant. And yet here I am thus quickly entering upon the enjoyment of it here and now in the present, when I am allowed to come right inside such a palace as this. Surely no one could attain the like except by the practice of the *Nembutsu*, as the Original Vow prescribed.

•

Details of the life were pared away to construct the essential: "Not this", "Not that." Worried about his state of mind, she made up a bed for herself on the living room floor and gave him her own bed. When he went into the bedroom he found he couldn't stay – there were photographs of other men, and letters he jealously examined, as well as posters which he couldn't help finding vulgar. He opened the door to the living room and said her name... and said that he had to leave. So she told him to turn the light on; and he let himself out. Once in the street, he equally couldn't face walking all the way home in the cold night. The samurai Saburō Tanemori came into contact with Hōnen when he was thirty-three and immediately became a disciple. After Hōnen died, Tanemori grew more and more sick of the world and wished to join Hōnen in Paradise. One night he slashed open his stomach and took out his entrails, wrapping them in a pair of silk trousers to be thrown into the river. She sat back in the chair, legs crossed, hands around her knee. Light on the right side of her face. – I shall never see you again, and you'll never know, nor will I.... They sat in silence for a time. Then she said: Will you take care of yourself? He looked away, at the white wall. After a while he said: You've had nothing to offer. Nothing except sentimental sympathy.... At the door there was nothing to say. In the subway he walked round and round, completely lost, unable to get a grip on himself. As he walked past the stream of people hurrying towards home from their jobs, he felt sick with remorse; as if the present state of his life were final.

Sources / Notes

Clothed with a Cloud:
"Then I saw an angel standing in the sun…": "The Revelation of St. John the Divine", 19:17 (*The Holy Bible*, King James Version). The Frederick van der Meer quotation is from the English version of his book *Apocalypse: Visions from the Book of Revelation in Western Art* (Thames and Hudson, 1978).

At the time the Dorothy and Benno stories were written, the singer Patty Waters had not recorded for many years, and did indeed seem the mysterious figure that she is made out to be in "Clothed with a Cloud" (and also in "Nightmare").

Biography:
Inspired by a Meredith Monk composition (of the same title). (Monk also refers to the piece as *The Dirge*.) "The blind spirit…": Abbot Suger of St. Denis, quoted by Stephen Bann in his essay "Brice Marden: From the Material to the Immaterial" (*Brice Marden: Paintings, Drawings and Prints*, Whitechapel Art Gallery, 1978).

Round About Midnight:
Named for the singer Karin Krog's idiosyncratic rendition (and titling) of Thelonious Monk's *Round Midnight*. Draws on legends concerning the Gnostic teacher Simon Magus. The quotation beginning "Separated from the person he loved…" is to do with John Ruskin, but I forget the source. *Skandhas*: in Buddhist thought, the constituents of the individual person (from which the belief in a "self" is formed). For Gurdjieff, see Whittall N. Perry's *Gurdjieff in the Light of Tradition* (Perennial Books, 1978).

Voice and Name:
Uses brief quotations from Shunjo's *Hōnen the Buddhist Saint:*

His Life and Teaching, translated by Rev. Harper H. Coates and Rev. Ryugaku Ishizuka (The Chion-in, 1925).

Blues:
The text draws on a mystical poem (in Latin) traditionally ascribed to Peter Damian, "The Beloved at the Door". The A. K. Coomaraswamy essay I refer to is entitled "The Sea"; the quotation is from Shams-i-Tabriz. (Roger Lipsey, ed., *Coomaraswamy: I. Selected Papers: Traditional Art and Symbolism*, Princeton University Press, 1977.)

The Serendipity Caper:
Draws on Marsilio Ficino, Giovanni Pico della Mirandola, Joachim of Fiore, Girolamo Savonarola and Georg Trakl. Brief quotations and paraphrases are taken from *The Letters of Marsilio Ficino*, vol. 1, translated anonymously (Shepheard-Walwyn, 1975), Edgar Wind, *Pagan Mysteries in the Renaissance* (Faber, 1958) (for a sentence of Pico's), and Bernard McGinn, ed., *Apocalyptic Spirituality* (SPCK, 1980). The Trakl quotation is from a letter to Ludwig von Ficker, and was located in Walter H. Sokel's *The Writer in Extremis: Expressionism in Twentieth-Century German Literature* (Stanford University Press /McGraw-Hill, 1964).

Dream Images of Life:
The stories of Naozane and Tanemori are derived from *Hōnen the Buddhist Saint* (see above). I've made use of quotations from letters and other documents.

D. M.
July 2005

Afterword:
FULL CIRCLE
by Anthony Rudolf

David Miller is so natural and unselfconscious as a writer that he gets away with being intellectual, that is to say he gets away with it in English, better yet (or worse yet) he gets away with it even in England, where such a way of being on the page is regularly taken as a pose, and the author as a poseur. I write with feeling, indeed with fellow feeling, after a plane journey on which my reading matter consisted of David's stories, obituaries of Derrida in English and French, notably in *Libération*, and certain philistine English reactions to Derrida published in *The Guardian* no less: these latter reminded me of the Momart fire after which similar or the same people derived pleasure from the destruction of artists' works.

My attempt at a reading of Miller's fictions – learned and playful, moving and laughter-inducing – involves thinking about what we mean by self-consciousness in a writer. Now, there is a sense in which all writing (even so-called automatic writing) is self-conscious. It can't be done by accident, it is deliberate, deliberated, although deliberation yields unintended surplus meanings in a first draft. One could attempt to conduct an investigation of this phenomenon, in Miller or more generally, under the sign of the late Derrida, for the man had the courage of his convictions and would have welcomed a good argument with him as an appropriate post-mortem homage, but such an investigation is beyond the scope of this essay and doubtless beyond the scope of this writer. Painting works differently but that too would be another essay.

David Miller cannot not know that it is *knowing* for a character (irrelevant whether or not the episode has a basis in David's own life) to be taken to meet David Jones in 1972, as indeed I was, oddly or not so oddly enough, although my trip was organised by John Montague. It is equally *knowing* on his part to incorporate into his stories all the many references to the arts, especially jazz. So, the writing is necessarily self-conscious in its execution and self-consciously intellectual in the choices made concerning what names to drop (in), what jazz numbers to include, which jokes or stories to tell or retell (I'd not heard the one about Charlie Parker and Sartre before).

So, how come I don't end up by withdrawing the word "unselfconscious" with which I started, and proceed along a new pathway or thread, or start again from scratch? Answer: because it is true and because what I wrote at the beginning is accurate. Even though the stories are full of conscious, indeed self-conscious choices, the writer himself is completely unselfconscious, at least to the extent that he doesn't give a brass monkey what the enemy thinks. He is being himself. His discourse is natural to him, musician and writer. His tone of voice is cool; the unexpected turns in the plot, the apparently false then righted moves, are redolent of improvisations familiar from bebop or swing standards. The trope of the detective is not peculiar to this author (see, for example, Auster, not to mention Keith Waldrop's "projective detective", his clever translation of Claude Royet-Journoud's "flic géometrique") but for the detective to be a musician in David's context is inspired, as is his use of space to evoke time – essential in fiction.

Yes, this is how David Miller plays the field. His field of play is that of a fabulist. It is my guess (based on fellow-feeling and affinity) that he is happier and freer as a poet and short story writer than as a writer of full-length novels: but, please note, this formulation is a joke since we all know that even a haiku is full length, as is an adult bee. In the kingdom of giants, a nine-foot girl is known as Thumbelina. Surely the

Melville of *Bartleby* and *Billy Budd,* not *Moby Dick* or *Pierre,* is his main man, ditto the Henry James of *The Middle Years* and *The Beast in the Jungle* not *The Bostonians* or *The Golden Bowl.* So, rephrase: "…a writer of long novels…."

For me to write "his discourse is natural to him" is a short-hand way of saying that he is an educated and learned writer, with deep experience and knowledge of another art, as a performer who improvises music if not as an Ellingtonian composer. Perhaps I am trying to say that David Miller's writing inhabits a parallel universe to that of music, or translates music into writing. Try again: music and writing (and not only in the sense of musical writing) interact dialectically in his mind, even in his brain: the synapses fire, the endorphins buzz, and the hive of mental activity generates the wild honey of his art.

A more straightforward way of approaching these marvellous stories would be to do a lit crit job on them but, in the words of Bartleby, I would prefer not to. What I hope I have succeeded in suggesting in this non-musician's amateur riff is that if David Miller with his learning and high culture and intellectuality comes across as unself-conscious and natural, it's because a master-musician is conducting his orchestra, or orchestrating his conduct.

OTHER TITLES IN PRINT FROM REALITY STREET EDITIONS:

POETRY SERIES
Kelvin Corcoran: *Lyric Lyric*
Maggie O'Sullivan: *In the House of the Shaman*
Susan Gevirtz: *Taken Place*
Allen Fisher: *Dispossession and Cure*
Denise Riley: *Mop Mop Georgette*
Fanny Howe: *O'Clock*
Maggie O'Sullivan (ed.): *Out of Everywhere*
Cris Cheek/Sianed Jones: *Songs From Navigation* (+ audio CD)
Nicole Brossard: *Typhon Dru*
Lisa Robertson: *Debbie: an Epic*
Maurice Scully: *Steps*
Barbara Guest: *If So, Tell Me*
Tony Lopez: *Data Shadow*
Denise Riley: *Selected Poems*
Anselm Hollo (ed. & tr.): *Five From Finland*
Lisa Robertson: *The Weather*
Robert Sheppard: *The Lores*
Lawrence Upton: *Wire Sculptures*
Ken Edwards: *eight + six*
Peter Riley: *Excavations*
David Miller: *Spiritual Letters (I-II)*
Allen Fisher: *Place*
Redell Olsen: *Secure Portable Space*
Tony Baker: *In Transit*

4PACKS SERIES
1: *Sleight of Foot* (M Champion, H Kidd, H Tarlo, S Thurston)
2: *Vital Movement* (A Brown, J Chalmers, M Higgins, I Lightman)
3: *New Tonal Language* (P Farrell, S Matthews, S Perril, K Sutherland)
4: *Renga+* (G Barker, E James/P Manson, C Kennedy)

FICTION SERIES
Ken Edwards: *Futures*
John Hall: *Apricot Pages*
David Miller: *The Dorothy and Benno Stories*

MEMOIR
Douglas Oliver: *Whisper 'Louise'*

Go to **www.realitystreet.co.uk**, email **info@realitystreet.co.uk**
or write to the address on the reverse of the title page for updates.

BECOME A REALITY STREET SUPPORTER!

Since 1998, more than 70 individuals and organisations have helped Reality Street Editions by being Reality Street Supporters. Those signed up to the current Supporter scheme, which runs till the end of 2006, are listed below (the list is correct at the time of going to press).

The Supporter scheme is an important way to keep Reality Street's programme of adventurous writing alive. As a Supporter, you receive all the press's titles free for three years. For more information, go to **www.realitystreet.co.uk** and click on the "About us" tab, or email **info@realitystreet.co.uk**

REALITY STREET SUPPORTERS, 2004-06:

Peter Barry
Charles Bernstein
Clive Bush
Richard Cacchione
CCCP
Adrian Clarke
Mark Dickinson
Michael Finnissy
Allen Fisher/Spanner
Sarah Gall
Chris Goode
John Hall
Alan Halsey
Robert Hampson
Peter Hodgkiss
Fanny Howe
Harry Gilonis &
　　Elizabeth James
Lisa Kiew
Peter Larkin
Tony Lopez
Ian McMillan
Richard Makin
Jules Mann
Mark Mendoza

Peter Middleton
Geraldine Monk
Maggie O'Sullivan
Marjorie Perloff
Pete & Lyn
Peter Philpott
Tom Quale
Peter Quartermain
Ian Robinson
Will Rowe
Susan Schultz
Maurice Scully
Robert Sheppard
John Shreffler
Peterjon & Yasmin Skelt
Hazel Smith
Valerie & Geoffrey Soar
Tony Trehy
Keith Tuma
Sam Ward
John Welch/The Many Press
John Wilkinson
Tim Woods
The Word Hoard
+ 8 anonymous